DRAGONMEAT

ANGELA BOORD

Impossible Books

For caregivers

PROLOGUE

WHAT DOES DRAGON TASTE LIKE?

That's what people whisper to me in the dark, so no one else will hear.

Does it taste like blood, all copper and salt?

Charred and burnt, like ash in your mouth?

Like chicken, some people joke.

But dragon tastes like the sky. Like an empty sea, with nothing between you and the horizon. Like the wind lifting you up and setting you soaring.

Dragon tastes like freedom.

CHAPTER 1

IT BEGAN WHEN A MAN CAUGHT ME STEALING FIGS in the market.

I didn't expect to be caught. I approached stealing the way I approached any other problem in my life—I studied it relentlessly. I would have used my Lyceum library privileges to make a review of the literature if there had been any. But unsurprisingly, the only scrolls I could find on thieving were philosophical treatises written by Eterean scholars who debated each other in marble salons while stuffing themselves with roast meats and sugared pies.

In other words, rubbish.

What I needed was evidence. Hard facts. So, I spent hours observing street children filch apples and almonds, bread and onions—sometimes even honey candies, though those went only to the bold. It was far easier to stick to the mundane. You were twice as likely to score a meal if no one noticed you, or if no one cared what you took.

In this, I was fortunate. I was just another small woman with olive skin, ragged dark hair, and a cloak full of holes. Not tall or pretty, no scars or distinguishing marks. Just... ordinary. Nobody ever looked twice at me. And I never attempted to steal anything flashy or rare. I would much rather get away with an onion than rot in prison because I had attempted to steal some meat.

But I couldn't resist the figs.

They were smuggled in on an illegal boat from somewhere warmer. The ones at the edge of the pile were soft and going bad. In a normal year, in any other place, they would have been fed to the pigs, and I could have had my pick without going to such desperate lengths.

But this wasn't a normal year, nor was it another place. This was Medeas, and everyone was starving.

A crowd jostled around the stall, poor wives and the servants of the rich all pushing and shoving to get at the rare delivery of produce. In such a mess, who would pay any attention to a girl in a tattered cloak, lurking in the back?

I darted through a gap between a big male slave and a large woman, both of them using their size to jostle smaller clients out of the way. But being small had its advantages. I shot into the middle of the crowd and grabbed a few squishy figs, then ducked under the table.

"Hey!" the male slave yelled, lunging toward me. "Come back here with those! Thief! Food thief!"

A cry rose as if the crowd had become a single animal—a hydra with hundreds of heads and arms. It swelled against the stall, despite the loud objections of the stall owner. I scuttled one way and then another, only to find my way blocked by more legs. The table wobbled, and figs spilled off the edge and bounced and splatted on the ground, releasing a sweet, spicy aroma that made my mouth water painfully.

"The figs!" a woman yelled and threw herself down, scooping handfuls of fruit toward her. They were so soft and pulpy they left a brown smear on the dirt, and the crowd paused for a moment, watching as this treasure threatened to be ground into a dusty paste. Then they all cast themselves down—scrambling for the spilled fruit, not caring whether they landed on a body or the ground.

I caught the woman's eye for the briefest of moments. Then a man smashed her into the dirt and pried the fruit out of her hands. More people landed on top of her, but even as she was being crushed beneath their weight, she struggled to lick the sweet, sticky mess from her fingers.

I shoved my stolen fruit into my pockets and wriggled out from under the table in the opposite direction. The mass of the crowd had shifted, piling onto the spilled figs. Soldiers clanked down the street, and metal dogs on chains at their sides— Eterean machines, powered by magic, that would be unleashed on the crowd if they couldn't keep the peace.

I clambered to my feet with my head down, preparing to walk off in the other direction. But before I could take a single step, a hand grabbed my collar and hauled me backward.

❧

"Let go of me!" I shouted. "I've done nothing!"

"So those figs you stole were nothing, were they?" The man who held me spoke quietly at my ear, his voice a strange counterpoint to the chaos— smooth and dark as Eterean silk.

I thrashed, trying to fight myself out of my cloak, but he'd clamped his fingers tight as a vice on the collar of my tunic, too. If he was one of Granthas's guards, I was done for.

"I don't know what you're talking about," I said in a haughty voice.

He laughed, more a movement in his chest than a sound. I wrenched around, preparing my plea of innocence, but the sight of him killed the words in my throat.

He wore a cloak with a hood covering hair that was white, not blond, though he didn't seem old enough for it. His skin was a youthful golden color, unmarred by wrinkles. And his eyes…

I supposed they could be called *hazel*, but *hazel* wouldn't have stood out in the darkness of a hood. They were a mix of green and gold and amber, tawny like a cat's and with a shine to them, as if they would gleam in the darkness like an animal's eyes. But the left was smashed at the corner, half-closed by scar tissue.

His mouth curved upward, more like the feral lips of a wolf pulling back to show its teeth than a real smile. "Get a good look?"

For a moment, I felt ashamed of the way I'd stared at him. Then I swallowed my shame and fear and forced myself to be rational. I'd never get out of here if I lost my head. "Pardon, ser," I said, in a voice I hoped sounded more polite than quavery. "I didn't mean to stare. But you surprised me so."

"I imagine I did. But if I let you go, somebody

from that crowd will think you're getting away with their food. Or the soldiers will find you."

"Me? But—"

"You underestimate the drive to survive. See what they've become? Animals. Just because they're hungry. One of them will give you away."

I met his eyes, stare for stare. "They could just as well accuse each other."

"I'm doing you a favor. Come on. Let's get out of here before somebody follows us."

❧

"They would have killed you, you know," he said once we were out of sight of the market. He let go of me and stepped back, and I got a better look at him.

With his hair, face, and eyes hidden by his hood, he seemed to disappear in the plain brown cloak—not tall or short, heavy or skinny. Slaves and the very poor perfected that ability, but his simple, neat green tunic and brown trousers marked him as a freeman.

I smoothed my own cloak as if I could ever make it more presentable. It was so full of holes it was barely a cloak anymore, and the long tunic I wore beneath it was hardly better. The red dye had faded until it was almost pink, and the wrapped leggings I wore underneath were ragged and more brown than cream-colored anymore. But like him I was of the free class, and not desperate enough to sell myself as a slave yet. My free clothes didn't make me stand out, so I continued to wear them with pride.

"I thought I could get away," I replied, discarding my fiction of protest—which I could now see was useless. "Because the crowd was focused on the figs. I made a study of the apple cart, when we had apples. Unless there was a guard devoted to protecting them, the children who acted normally almost always succeeded in stealing an apple. It was the ones whose fear bested them, who couldn't wait and then ran, who were caught. I kept track, in my notes."

He stared at me for a moment. Then he laughed. "You took notes?"

"Well. I wasn't going to undertake a risky venture like thieving without basing my strategy on evidence. That would have been suicide."

"Why did you risk the figs then? Didn't you hear about the food riot down on the docks?"

"I heard about the riots," I said stiffly.

"You heard how they were put down?"

"By Granthas's soldiers and his machines? Of course."

Granthas was the governor of Medeas,

appointed by the Emperor in Eterea itself. He was the man tasked with protecting us, and he took his job very seriously.

"So even after hearing about that massacre... you started your own riot by stealing a rotten fig?"

He was right. I shouldn't have risked it. Figs were much too rare. Everyone wanted one. But I wasn't about to admit the real reason I had tried to steal a fig.

I fluffed out my cloak and sniffed. "It wasn't really a *riot*, was it?"

"What would you call it then? A disagreement?"

"You said it yourself. It's the drive to survive. Aren't we all hungry?"

He watched me for a moment with a measuring look. Then he reached inside his cloak and took out a rectangular packet of undyed muslin. He unwrapped it slowly, corner by corner, revealing a piece of bread.

He took a big, slow bite out of it.

Saliva sprang into my mouth so quickly and intensely it hurt. My belly tightened in pain. I could smell it from here—that fragrant, yeasty perfume that made me want to cry out for want of it. I fought back the urge to rip the bread from his hands. When he opened his mouth for a second bite, I couldn't take it anymore.

"Stop!" I shouted, putting my hands out.

His eyebrows rose, twin arches a much darker color than his hair. Silently, he held the bread out, in a gesture for me to come get it.

"And the muslin, too," I said.

"You can't eat muslin."

"It's not for me."

"Ah." He rocked back on his heels. "I didn't think so. A girl desperate enough to spark a riot by stealing a fig should have been eating it under the table, not saving it for later."

"Are you still going to give me the bread?" I asked.

He held it out to me silently.

I stepped forward to take it, then stopped. "Why are you so willing? Is there a price attached? Are you an acolyte from the Dragon Temple, trying to tempt me away with you?"

His hand remained outstretched. "I feel like I'm trying to tame a problem horse."

"Forgive me, but I need evidence to trust a man who just dragged me into an alley."

He lowered the bread. "And you'd believe me if I set you a price? If that's the case, how about your time? Meet me at the Tavern-By-the-Walls tomorrow night."

I laughed out loud. "And you expect me to believe all you want is my time? I'm sorry, but there's no evidence for that either."

"Well, if I wanted something else, I'd just take it, wouldn't I? I could hold this bread up and make you beg like a dog."

"Beg like a dog," I repeated, as if it were the most ridiculous thing I'd ever heard.

He eyed me curiously. "Wouldn't you?"

I wanted to say no, but I think he saw the truth on my face. I *would* beg, because the bread wasn't for me. I flushed hot anyway, then pressed my mouth shut tight.

He flicked his wrist and tossed the bread to me with barely a motion. I lunged for it, caught it in both hands, and fought the urge to drop to my knees and rescue the falling crumbs.

"I'm not asking you to bed me," he said. "You're a bit of a scruffy pick-up anyway, aren't you?"

I flushed even redder. I had made myself scruffy on purpose, but it embarrassed me to be reminded of it. "Are you done insulting me?" I said.

"I'm not sure how else I can reassure you. Except by insults. If I spoke to you politely, you'd use it as evidence I was trying to get something out of you. But all I want is for you to meet me at the gates."

"Why?"

"Because I want to show you something. This isn't the first time I've watched you steal food only to shove it in your pockets."

"You've been *watching* me?"

That drew a real smile out of him. "You're not the only one with powers of observation. I hang around the markets. I see what goes on. You've got light fingers. One might call you a professional food thief."

"There are lots of people on the streets who could be called the same."

"Most of them eat their spoils right away. But you... you've got willpower."

"Like you, do you mean? You're not stealing food, you're giving it away."

"I don't need willpower," he said as his smiled widened. For some reason, it didn't seem like a human smile. It was more dangerous. More... carnivorous. "I'm not hungry."

WE IN MEDEAS HAD BEEN LIVING UNDER FAMINE conditions for a long time. A few dry years, and the wheat fields withered, the grape vines burnt, the grass that the sheep grazed on died. But the drought couldn't account for everything. There was money in the coffers. We could have bought our food from the mainland.

But Granthas barred ships from entering or

leaving the harbor. Our city had walls, but cliffs and the sea formed our real prison.

Granthas had quarantined us because of the dragons. To prevent them from destroying Empire ships and disrupting Empire trade. To stop them killing Empire citizens.

We were not citizens. We were only provincials.

"How are you not hungry?" I said in amazement.

"Meet me at the gates," the man said. "If you want to find out."

He turned to go. He had an odd gait, shambling, like he was dragging one of his feet.

"Wait!" I called. "How will I find you? What if I miss you?"

He stopped and turned his head imperceptibly. "Just ask the barkeep for Frost."

CHAPTER 2

WHEN HE HAD GONE, I HURRIED HOME. OR TO what passed as home.

It was only a chilly basement room beneath a house packed as tightly with families as a roll of sardines. Above us, babies cried and children laughed and squabbled, and women fought with and loved their husbands, who hung around the plaza out front and played cards because with no ships, there was little work. The smell of frying oil always hung about the place, even though all anybody was frying were thin cakes of flour and water, sometimes stretched with sawdust and clay.

The piece of bread Frost gave me might as well have been gold. But only a man whose stomach was full could think gold more valuable than bread. I knew better.

I clattered down the stairs and fumbled the key out of my cloak, shoved it in the door, and disappeared inside as fast as I could. All the way back, I felt like somebody was watching me, just waiting to steal my food. I slammed the door shut and locked it.

"Peri?" a weak voice called from from a pile of blankets on the floor in the corner of the room.

"Papa!" I exclaimed.

I ran to him and fell on my knees. He lay in a fetal position, his legs drawn up to his chest. Once, he had been a big man, like a bear. Maybe that had just been a girl's perspective. But ever since That Morning he had shrunk. I couldn't help thinking of the day he'd been struck down by his disease as a proper noun, though I suppose to the rest of Medeas, it had been a normal spring day—pleasant, blue-skied and cool. For us it marked the division between life as it was and our new, topsy-turvy existence, in which people said he'd become a shadow of himself. But a shadow was wispy, filmy, ethereal. My father was still corporeal, but he had bent and withered like a tree dying from drought.

His mouth drooped on the right side. When he said *Peri*, the sound came out mushy and reedy. He couldn't lift his right hand to eat, to comb his hair, to wash. When he tried to walk, his right foot gave under him, tumbling him to the floor.

"What happened?" I said. "Did you try to get up by yourself? Where was Yula?"

"Yula," he repeated, confused.

"The girl above. I gave her a bowl of noodles so she would check on you."

My father's face was pinched against the dirt of the cellar floor, but now his brows cleared. "The girl. Left. Can get up myself."

"Dammit," I said, getting my arm underneath his. "You know you need help. Why didn't you wait for me?"

"Peranza. Watch. Your. Mouth."

Sometimes when our roles went back the right way, it made me want to cry. "Yes, sir," I said. I pulled hard on his arm, dragging him up. "Onto the bed again with you."

He made a sound; I couldn't tell what it meant. I helped him to the cot in the corner and sat him down on it, and he sighed as he leaned against the wall. Then he patted my knee with his left hand.

"Peri," he said again. He said my name a lot. Maybe he needed to remind himself of who I was. "Good girl."

"I've brought you some figs, Papa. Your favorite. And some bread."

He looked surprised. "Where? The markets have?"

I smiled tightly and nodded. "The markets

have." I stretched out my hand and uncurled my fingers to reveal the bread Frost had given me.

My father looked at me. His eye pulled down on the right side, too. I remembered when his hair had been as dark as mine, his features as chiseled as if they were hewn from wood. Now they drooped as if they were made of wax, and his hair and beard revealed the gray that had been lurking there, for years maybe, while I carried on, thinking he was ageless.

"Peri? You ate?" my father said.

I forced the smile to remain. "Yes," I lied. "I ate."

Slowly, clumsily, he took the bread with his left hand and tore off a piece with his teeth. Crumbs dribbled over his lips and stuck in his beard, but he didn't seem to notice.

I brushed them away. "We'll need to trim your beard again soon."

"Crazy old man," he said, with a wheeze that was supposed to be a laugh. "Mistake me for a wizard."

I laughed. He tried harder to smile, but his mouth only turned upward on the left side. The events of the marketplace left me no defenses against my emotions. I felt like crying, but that isn't what Papa would have done if the situation was reversed.

Papa would have made tea.

He had made a lot of tea for my sister and me. Bad things happened to us, small things, little girl things—things a mother should have dealt with—but since there wasn't any mother, he took them as seriously as if they meant the world.

That does sound like a difficult problem. Why don't I make tea and we'll talk about it.

I rose to putter around with the kettle and the fire in the brazier we used for both warmth and cooking. I'd banked the fire when I left, and now I poked it again to get it going. It was late fall, and winter was just beginning to send out its icy heralds. In a better year, we would have had barrels of apples, and I would have come home to make pies or dumplings, or perhaps to bake an apple for each of us, drizzling them with honey and almonds, and just a dash of cinnamon...

Reluctantly, I pulled myself from my fantasies and reached into my pocket for our reality, two half-spoiled figs, one of which was smashed into the fabric of my pocket. I set them on the table, trying not to drool. In truth, I should have stuck to onions. But Papa had always loved figs—fig cakes, fig jam—and I had thought, if only I brought him a fig, maybe it would lighten this dark basement a little. But what had I got for indulging in flights of fancy? A riot and a man who now knew I was a thief.

Useless to worry about that now. What's done was done, no matter how much I might regret it. I could only chalk it up as a lesson of what not to do in the future. I went back to the shelf and began searching through all the jars and pots with their clearly lettered labels, looking for some combination of herbs that would make my fingers stop trembling.

A nice chamomile was what I needed.

When I turned around, Papa was half-asleep, leaning against the wall. He'd used to possess so much energy, reading and writing long into the night, sketching new plants he'd found on his hikes into the mountains. Everything was fodder for his research.

"Papa?" I said. "Would you like me to read the letter from Vri while you eat your figs?"

"Read," he sighed, closing his eyes again. "But you eat."

"Papa, the figs were for you."

"Not hungry."

Whatever remaining integrity I'd possessed felt like it fell through the bottom of my stomach. I'd caused a riot, and all for nothing. I wanted to argue with him, but I probably wouldn't get anything else to eat today.

So, I pushed the thoughts away, sat at the table, and picked up the sheaf of papers lying there. It was the last letter from my sister before Granthas closed the port. My father asked me to read it over and over, almost as often as he asked me to read from his botany books.

"*Dear Papa and Peri,*" I read. "*I have settled into Eterea as well as might be expected for such a provincial. Honestly, if I hear one more person disparage us as an outpost of barbarians, I think I shall vomit. An extra vomit shouldn't be hard to work in, considering vomiting is the thing I am most prepared to do these days, especially if there is any savory meat in the vicinity. This little one thinks he can subsist entirely on honey buns and cheese curds. Thank the gods Breus is willing to have them brought to me at any hour of day or night. I must confess it strange, having servants to provide me with such odd requests. I've startled more than one kitchen maid in the early dark, coming in to start the fire only to find me sitting in my nightdress and robe, eating cheese straight out of the pot with my fingers.*"

"How old?" Papa said.

I sighed, turning a fig in my fingers until they grew sticky. I put the fig down and licked away the sweetness, savoring the taste with every swipe of my tongue. "The baby will have been born by now," I said when my fingers were clean. "Maybe even toddling around."

Thank the gods Vri's new husband had taken her off the island before Granthus went mad. I'd seen starving pregnant women. Their bellies continued to swell, but they looked like a ball attached to a pile of sticks.

"Peri. Eat."

I let out a deep sigh and lifted the fig to my mouth, closing my eyes in the hopes it would be possible for me to enjoy it. But the first bite was so sweet it was painful, and all I could see as I squeezed the seedy pulp between my teeth was the woman on the ground, licking her fingers while she was being crushed by the men on her back.

"Where," Papa said.

I swallowed and opened my eyes. Papa sat hunched over, watching me intensely. He looked like a vulture, wrapped in his blanket with his shoulders pulled up, his dark eyes feverishly bright.

"Bread. Where?" he said.

"I told you, I got it in the market—"

"No ovens."

So now your mind works? I thought testily and immediately regretted it. Guilt washed over me. I pushed the other fig aside.

"A man gave it to me."

"Peri—begging?"

"No! I would never beg, Papa."

"Money?"

If I could have lied to him, I would have. But he knew our dwindling supply of herbs had shrunk to the point where it was mostly unsellable. Just a few pots and jars left for making tea. No ability to get out of the city to replenish our stores, no way to write to foreign countries, asking for more. An herbalist with no herbs went out of business quickly.

"No," I said.

"Then... what?"

I ran my thumb up and down the handle of my teacup. "He asked me for my time. He said to come see him at the city gates tomorrow."

Papa tried to shake his head. "Bad bargain."

I cupped my tea in both hands and stared into it as if I were a truthseer, mostly to avoid looking at Papa. I knew I'd made a bad bargain. I only half-believed Frost when he said he had no interest in trading food for sex, even though I hoped it was truth. But I'd made that bed, and now I would need to lie in it.

"Stay," Papa said.

"But he might have more bread."

Papa's left brow pulled down, and a dark flush spread over his face. "Peranza. You, one of *those* girls? For bread?" He shook his head, as violently as he could manage. "Not *my* bread. Not *my* girl. No. *No.*"

I didn't like how red he was turning. I put my cup down, and by the time I stepped to the side of the bed, he'd started choking—gasping and gulping for breath, but still shaking his head and saying, "No, *no*!"

His limbs tremored and jerked. I put my arms around him, tight, trying to stop it. "Papa. Hush. It's all right. I won't become one of *those* girls. Don't worry. It will be all right. *Hush*."

Slowly, his body lost its rigidity. He slumped in my arms and began to cry on my shoulder—not really any tears, just dry sounds.

My life was like one of those trick pictures painted by Eterean artists. Look at it your whole life and see only one thing, as if the painting contained but a single image. Then one day someone flips the painting over, and you realize it forms an entirely new picture when you turn it upside down. You can never go back to seeing the first picture the way it was. Now all you've got is the upside-down painting.

How much longer could this go on? How much longer could we live this way, on stolen figs and bread?

CHAPTER 3

My father wasn't afraid I would become a prostitute—at least not a common one.

He wanted to save me from becoming a Dragon Girl.

The heart of Medeas was the Dragon Temple, dedicated to an old god whose name no one remembered anymore. Next to the temple were the Offices of the Governor, which Granthas now occupied, the Office of Sedition, and the Lyceum, where the free and noble classes of the island were educated. The round towers and flat roof of the Temple, built of native timber and red and black basalt, jutted up out of the jumble of foreign marble buildings constructed by the Etereans like the volcano that thrust itself cloudward on the northern side of the island.

We had always been dedicated to our dragons—dedicated to them even as we feared them. The entire island was said to have once been a dragon, tamed and cursed by the father god Tekus when he claimed control of the sea. But when the Etereans came, our relationship with dragons changed.

Before the Etereans, Dragon Fixers magicked our populations of dragons into leaving us alone. It didn't always work, but after the Etereans the Dragon Fixers began to fail. So, the Etereans turned to the Dragon Youth.

The Dragon Youth were magic attractors—young men and women who drew magic to themselves like a lodestone captured iron. Acolytes from the Dragon Temple trolled the neighborhoods, luring in poor girls and boys with promises of food and shelter to take the Temple's magic tests. The youth who passed these tests served as sacred courtesans to the governor's Fixers, to soak up as much magic as possible.

Then they became a lodestone for dragons. The dragons feasted on the Dragon Youth and left the rest of the city alone.

But Frost didn't seem the acolyte type, even if he had wielded his bread like a hunter baiting a trap. The acolytes always dressed in rich patrician robes of purple and indigo, not plain freeman clothes like Frost had. And when they came into the poorer areas of town, they looked down their proud Eterean noses at us. Still, I tried to talk myself out of meeting him. I listed all the sane and sensible reasons it would be dangerous to go. I told myself I would be violating the spirit of the discussion I'd had with my father.

If I'd made a promise to him, I would have abided by it. But as with my decision to become a thief, hunger and my father's well-being became their own justification. Watching Papa wrestle again with scrolls he'd once read and written with ease... as my hunger pangs kept me awake that night on my own thin pallet on the floor, listening to his heavy, labored breathing... I turned our words over in my head until I realized I hadn't promised him anything. He'd only said he didn't want me to become a Dragon Girl. Once I'd discovered this loophole, I couldn't help but walk through it.

If Frost *was* from the Dragon Temple, it wouldn't matter, anyway. I was far too ordinary to pass the magic tests. I didn't know why Papa worried so much.

In the morning, I ransacked our paltry stores for an old turnip and a shriveled carrot I'd snitched from a food cart two days ago. I chopped them into a pot of water and threw in a few grains of salt and set it to boil, then smashed the remains of my fig together with the leftover crumbs of bread into a tiny cake. My father seemed to be having a good day, which meant he was sitting up, making another attempt to read an old set of his notes. I glimpsed a sketch of a woman mixed in with the papers—lots of wild dark hair, the sly corner of a smile, an official stamp in the corner.

My mother.

He'd be absorbed in his task for a long time, then. When I was younger, I'd rarely seen that sketch of my mother, but now he looked at it every day—almost as often as he studied his portrait of Vri. Watching him trace the lines of their pictures with the fingers of his left hand, made me ache in a complicated way. I missed Vri. I told myself I didn't miss my mother, but maybe I did, deep inside.

I hadn't found a study yet that would sort out those emotions.

Papa barely noticed when I slipped outside with the fig cake, such as it was, and snuck upstairs to ask Yula to stay with him again. I had to rap hard on her door to get anyone to answer it. Yula lived with her large family—parents, siblings, nieces and nephews, cousins, lovers, friends—the gods only knew the relationships of all the people who passed over that threshold. I couldn't imagine living in the middle of such constant noise and chaos, but when I went back downstairs to the small room I shared with my father, it felt so empty and quiet, so... invisible. If I disappeared, who would miss me? Just my father. Then again, if I went missing, my father would die; if Yula went missing, her family would just close ranks.

Thinking about it that way should have made me feel better—more necessary. Instead, I felt like somebody had shoved me underwater and told me to breathe. What I wouldn't give, just for a day, to be like Yula—surrounded by capable people, loved, noticed... and utterly unnecessary.

Except that *I* needed her. Who else could I get to sit with a sick old man?

She finally came to the door. Her round, brown face was flushed from the heat of the crowded room, and she was smiling until she saw me. Then her gaze slid backward over her shoulder, and she slid out the door, pulling it almost closed behind her, her fingers in the crack the only thing keeping it open. With her other hand, she threw her long tail of black curls over her shoulder and leaned toward me.

"You want me to watch your papa again, yes?"

Yula had grown up down on the docks. She had a sailor's lilt to her speech, a remnant of not so long ago when our docks welcomed the whole world. But now her father had no work, and his family's speech was just a footnote in history—or it would be, if any of us survived to write the story.

"You'll pay me again today, yes?" she said.

I opened my hand to reveal the fig cake. Yula flushed and squealed in delight. "Oh, fig!" she said, and swiped the cake off my palm. She put the whole thing in her mouth and closed her eyes.

"I have soup on the boil, too," I said. "It's only water now, so you'll have to stay until it's done if you want to eat."

She opened her eyes and looked at me with the crumbs of the cake still dusting her lips. She swallowed and licked them away before she spoke. "Hard to carry soup," she said.

I sighed. "I know. Have the little ones down if you like. Papa would enjoy that."

"Oh, Ma don't want me down there in the first place. Thinks what your papa has is catching. But maybe..." She glanced up at me shyly, from under her sparse eyelashes, "I could bring my man?"

I eyed her skeptically. "Is that what happened yesterday, Yula? Is that why you left Papa alone?"

"Oh, no, sera," she said hurriedly. "No, *ma'am*." She looked down sheepishly. "It was the little ones, you know. Ma don't like me down there, and one of the little ones said Ma was looking for me, and well —all them lovely noodles would have gone to waste. So, I had to come up and tell Ma a lie and then the little ones got the noodles, and oh, sera, you should have seen their faces."

I shifted uncomfortably. "Well, I still don't know about bringing a *man*..."

"You can meet him," Yula said happily. Before I could stop her, she pushed open the door and called, "Bero! Come here, won't you?"

A tall, thin man wearing a burgundy tunic walked over. Like everyone else, he looked like he was wearing clothes too big for him, and the hollows in his cheeks made his nose even more prominent. His brown curls formed a tight cap on top of his head.

Yula folded her hands over his arm, and he leaned forward in expectation of being introduced. "This is Peri," she said. "She lives downstairs. Her Papa is sick and needs tending. I thought you might come with me and help. Perhaps her papa would like a little male company—though he can't speak much. Can read and write, though. Used to be a scholar."

"Aye?" the man said, with genuine interest. "What kind of scholar was he?"

"Botany," I said. "If it matters. Really, it was nice to meet you, but I need to be going—"

"I'm a scribe," he said. "Down at the Office of Sedition. All I do is copy out writs. Was a time I thought I might be trained in the Lyceum." He gave me a wistful smile, and Yula patted his arm.

"It's a good job," she said. "Working as a copyist. We might be able to have our own room some day."

"I get more work all the time," he said. "What with the Seditionists getting more and more active. I wrote ten condemnations yesterday alone."

"Ten!" I exclaimed.

The Seditionist party was outlawed by the Empire. You heard murmurs about them in the market, sometimes saw bits of their rhetoric copied out on scraps of paper passed around taverns and back alleys by men who thought we could overpower Granthus and his Eterean Guard if we would only band together. The Etereans came down ruthlessly on Seditionists if they caught them, throwing them to their vicious machine monsters for entertainment if they weren't executed outright. The Seditionists mainly laid low. Ten condemnations in one day was a lot.

Yula's man looked at me with solemn, hangdog eyes. "If you don't mind me saying so, sera, I'd be careful going out today. The food riot yesterday got people stirred up, and the Seditionists are trying to work the crowd, so to speak. It's not safe."

I hoped he didn't notice the way I tensed. "Surely, just going out..."

"You don't even want to be seen in contact with them. The guards have been picking up everyone, hoping to stamp out the movement now before it gains momentum. They bring everybody in, then sort them out later."

"But you... you've nothing to do with the Governor, do you?" I asked hesitantly. "Or the guards? You just copy writs?"

He gave me a strange look, then laughed. "No, I'm not important enough to deal with the Governor's Office. I've basic copying skills, that's it. Why? Is your business with the Governor's Office?"

He turned curious eyes on me, and I made myself put on a bland smile, reminding myself of the most important precept I had learned from thieving: *Act like you're not breaking any rules.* "No," I said. "I was just curious. I suppose it would be all right to bring him, Yula."

But my stomach had knotted up so much that for once all thoughts of eating flew from my head. I wasn't cut out for thievery, or sneakery, or intrigue. I would have been happiest to have set up our apartment in an unused corner of the Lyceum laboratory. I missed the surety of droppers and vials, mortars and pestles. But I reminded myself that all this— meeting Frost, making sure Yula's man was safe— was for my father.

It wouldn't do me any good to venture into the dragon's lair, if I allowed the dragon into ours.

THE CITY GATES LOOMED UP OUT OF THE FOGGY morning like a doorway to another time. My ancestors had built them long ago, and the story of the island was carved into their basalt pillars. All of that history was lost now to Eterean rule, buried in Eterean construction projects, which had ground to a halt when the dragons returned and Granthus closed the harbor.

A contingent of Eterean soldiers guarded the gates to make sure no one entered or left. There seemed to be a lot of them around this morning. Some of the soldiers wore the impassive wooden masks and bells our Dragon Fixers used long ago to signify their authority over the dragons. It wasn't clear if the Eterean soldiers wore them to scare the dragons or to scare us. The machine dogs at their sides seemed to indicate the latter. The gold trim on many of the uniforms made me nervous; only Granthus's private bodyguard wore Eterean gold, and Granthus wasn't the sort of governor who remained shut up in his palace. He had been a general before he was made governor, and he still maintained his military habits.

I dodged a soldier to enter the Tavern-By-the-Walls—a squat, sturdy building made of the same basalt as the gates. A mill with a great water wheel shared a wall with it, and the creak and splash of the wheel as the stream turned it soon swallowed the sound of the soldier's clanking bells as he walked away.

I pushed the door to the tavern open quickly before I lost my nerve.

Inside, it should have smelled like breakfast. Instead, it smelled like onions and frying fish and whatever bad beer people were brewing using old, moldy grain. People still gathered, though—men mostly, sitting at the tables and nursing their mugs, gaunt faces flushed with the warmth of the fire, or maybe the effects of alcohol on empty stomachs.

I tried to pretend I belonged and walked straight up to the barkeep.

He looked up from wiping out a mug and raised an eyebrow at me. "Sera?" he said. "What can I get you?"

"I'm—I'm here to meet someone. His name is Frost."

The eyebrow only crept further upward. "Frost, eh."

"Yes," I said, trying to recollect my confidence. Or maybe to invent it. "He told me to meet him here. If he isn't around, I could leave him a note. Or... or I could wait. But I can't wait long."

"I'm sure he wouldn't want you to wait."

I jerked my head up to see Frost himself walking through a door behind the bar. He still wore his cloak and hood. He put a hand on the barkeep's shoulder. "Tea, I think, and whatever food you've got."

"Ain't much, Frost."

"Just bring it to the table in the back."

He led me to an empty table in the back corner, and a serving girl brought us steaming cups of tisane—an herbal concoction, not exactly tea.

I sniffed before I drank. "Clover," I sighed, wrapping my cold hands around the mug. "Well, at least it's not dandelion. All we need now is to have our appetites stimulated. But the clover should be all right."

"It grows on the hillside behind us."

"If we were all sheep, we'd be fine."

His mouth twisted into that amused, cynical smile I remembered from yesterday. "If we were sheep that eat grass, I suppose. Have you come for the bread?"

"Why else would I be here?"

"Did you eat the figs?"

"I ate... one fig."

"Have you had anything else since yesterday?"

"What do you think?"

"I'm just wondering why a woman wearing free-man's clothes has been reduced to stealing food she doesn't even eat."

I took a sip of the tisane and settled the mug back on the table firmly before leaning toward him.

"And I wonder where that food's coming from. And why you would want to talk to *me*."

He waved his hand vaguely. "The food's coming from out of the gates."

"You're a smuggler? But aren't they starving outside, too?"

"Not everyone outside is starving. But I'm not a smuggler. And I'm not sharing the names of my sources. How about we start with your name first?"

"Peri," I told him curtly.

"Just 'Peri'? You're a freewoman. There's more to it than that."

"Peranza," I said, sighing.

He gave me the same odd look most everyone did, but unlike most people he didn't immediately proclaim its strangeness. My full name was the least ordinary thing about me, given to me by hopelessly scholarly parents. "My parents liked poetry," I said apologetically.

Frost smiled. "Peranza the Steadfast. The goddess of fortune dropped a skein of yarn she received from the fatespinners. Peranza found it and wouldn't rest until she returned it."

"You've read it." I was surprised. The story merited a brief mention in a long poem about the war of the gods over the province of magic. My parents had shared a poetry tutor at the Lyceum and fallen in love while memorizing stanzas. My name was but a lingering memory of a love that had been dead for a long time.

Frost shrugged. "Heard it read. Does Peranza the Steadfast have a family name?" He watched me with those oddly flecked animalian eyes, which grew more hooded the longer my silence spun out. But I wasn't about to give him my family name if I could help it.

"How do you get out of the gates?" I asked. "Without the soldiers catching you? Do you bribe them? Feed them?"

He snorted. "The soldiers have food. You're the one who needs it."

He turned his gaze directly on me. The shadows of his hood seemed to lend his eyes even greater intensity. I thought I had imagined their strangeness, but I was wrong. They were just as not-quite-human as I remembered. Was it only the color or also the shape of his pupils? Or maybe it was the fact that even while he spoke words of compassion, his eyes were hard as polished agate.

I was staring. I turned away, embarrassed.

"I'm fine," I said. "But my father..."

Mid-sentence the tavern door opened and a group of soldiers dressed in masks and bells walked in. They announced their entrance with a jangle and clang, and everyone in the room looked up.

"The Most Esteemed Governor Granthus," an unmasked soldier announced. "All rise."

I thought I heard Frost curse softly, but maybe it was just the murmur that ran through the room as the men pushed back their chairs and stood up. *I* wanted to curse. Granthus wouldn't recognize me by sight. But he knew my family, and I didn't want to invite any attention to my father, if we were questioned in a search for Seditionists. I wished, suddenly, that I'd listened to Yula's copyist and stayed home.

Granthus stood ramrod straight in the doorway, his deep burgundy cape secured over his shoulders with golden pins that gleamed in the yellow light. The light also flashed off the golden wolf's head stitched on his tunic. His silver hair swept down from a high widow's peak and lay clean and soft against his back. He looked something like his machines, Fixed by Smiths from precious metals. He began to remove his black gloves.

"My lord," the barkeep said. "To what do we owe this visit?"

"I was inspecting the gates again. Now I desire breakfast for myself and my men."

The barkeep looked up nervously at the soldiers crowding the entrance. "My lord. There are too many of them."

"What do you mean, too many?"

"Forgive me, but we don't have enough food."

"Aren't you a tavern? I've eaten here many times before."

"Yes, my lord, but... we've had no deliveries since Ninth Month."

"Haven't I put out edicts that the city shall become self-sufficient?" Granthus said testily. "We've the sea. You can raise rabbits, can't you? Fowl? Grow vegetables in pots?"

One of the men standing at a table near the door broke in. "If it wasn't nearly winter."

Granthus swung around. "Who said that?"

The man squared his shoulders. He looked as if he'd been bigger in the past, the way his clothes hung off his shoulders. His curly black beard had gray streaks in it. "I did, my lord."

"You're using autumn as an excuse? You could have turned to this work a month ago instead of waiting for deliveries."

"Takes time to grow things, my lord, and it's too cold now. Besides, wheat don't grow in a pot. Where are we to get our bread?"

A low rumble of agreement spread through the men at the tables.

"We *all* have to tighten our belts in these hard times," Granthus said. "But I expect you to feed your protectors."

"Protectors?" the man burst out. "The dragons never killed this many people!"

Dead silence.

Granthus pulled on the glove he'd removed. "Take him," he told his soldiers.

The man broke. His shoulders, held proudly a moment before, slumped and he looked around wildly. He grabbed a table knife and whipped it out in front of him. But he was no match for trained Eterean guards. They grabbed him and dragged him out the door.

In the brief lacuna that followed, while everyone wondered what to do, I looked at Frost. He was carving marks on the table with his thumbnail, not watching the proceedings at all.

He was an Acolyte or a Seditionist, and I didn't want to associate with either. When the rest of the men ran out of the room to watch what happened to their compatriot, I whirled and ran, too.

"Peri!" Frost called out. I heard him throw a chair out of the way to follow me, but I didn't stop.

I didn't stop to watch the man being savaged in the courtyard either—torn apart by snarling, silver dogs while the soldiers laid down money and Granthus stood by with his arms crossed over his chest.

Instead, I lost myself in the crowd and ran all the way home.

CHAPTER 4

I laid low for a while. But we had to eat.

Every time I went out, the feeling of being watched crawled over my back. Sometimes I even turned fast enough to see white hair poking out of a hood. I began to avoid our marketplace and instead walked all the way down to the fish markets. It was a lot harder to steal a big, slimy fish than it was to pocket a couple of figs, though. The smell always gave you away.

Soldiers roamed all over the city now. They wore their stern wooden masks, the strings of bells slung over their shoulders a clanging, jangling cacophony with every step. I barely dared steal anything, and what I did, I gave to my father.

Then one day, I found myself wandering the street in front of the Dragon Temple.

I didn't know how my feet brought me there. Maybe I'd walked that direction to avoid a familiar brown hood or a flip of white hair—or maybe that was just a dream. My hunger had passed the point of pain and propelled me into a perpetual light-headed fugue state.

Eating cheese straight out of the pot with my fingers, I read from Vri's letter, and I couldn't even imagine such a thing. Did cheese exist? Was there once a time when we could have it any time we wanted it, and sit at a table in the middle of the night, eating it with our fingers?

By some kind of hunger logic, I wondered if Frost had been herding me toward the Temple. Maybe he *was* an acolyte. After all, he'd ignored the suffering of the Seditionist in the tavern. If I found Frost at the temple, perhaps all our problems would be solved. I'd be fed until I failed the magic tests, Vri was safe in Eterea where the Temple couldn't find her, and for the brief time they let me stay, surely the temple would take care of my father.

Hunger spins a dangerous rhetoric.

The thought let something loose inside me, though. Something that was holding me up, making me put one foot in front of the other. I'd found myself woolgathering in front of the Temple before, but this time an acolyte pushed open the big oak doors and stepped onto the portico. It wasn't Frost, and for some reason this surprised me. I don't know why I'd convinced myself it would be him. But this acolyte was Eterean, with that classic patrician nose that looked as if it had been broken in the middle, and curly brown hair and olive skin just a shade lighter than my own. The sleeves of his rich red wool robes were so voluminous he could run his hands up them, which he did.

"Can I help you, girl?"

Could he help me? My heart pounded in my chest. My ribs felt light as bird bones, and my heart skipped beats as its pace quickened.

"Is there a man here?" I said. "With white hair? A young man, not an old one?"

The acolyte frowned. Then he lifted his head slightly, the frown turning into a crafty look. "Are you talking about Stefan Frost?"

Stefan. So that was his real name. I bobbed my head. "Perhaps you could fetch him?"

The acolyte barked a laugh. "If I could do that, girl, I'd likely get a promotion. What do you know about Frost?" He gave me a look with an edge to it, like a knife.

I stumbled backward. "N-nothing," I said. "I thought he might be an acolyte—"

The acolyte tilted his head. He reminded me of a bird of prey. But then his expression turned prospective, and in an instant, his face smoothed over with benevolence, as if he had suddenly donned a mask. He leaned toward me.

"So, you wanted to enter the Temple?"

"I—" I stuttered. "I don't know."

"Oh," he said. "But, look at how your bones stand out. And how thin your hair is. You're hungry, aren't you?"

Mutely, I nodded.

"Poor girl. Life is hard on the streets, isn't it? Perhaps you need a bed. And a bath? And supper, of course. We've supper every night."

Every night? I wanted to say, like a little girl asking about candies. Instead I said, "How?"

The acolyte pulled one of his hands out of his sleeves and waved it vaguely in the air. "Sacrifices are made elsewhere to provide food for the Dragon Youth. Saving the populace from dragon attack is a very important role."

"Y-yes," I said unsteadily.

The acolyte removed his other hand from his sleeves. In his fingers he held a small, shriveled brown thing. A date. He held it up so I could see.

"Would you like to come inside? There's something familiar about you... what did you say your name was?"

"Peri," I breathed, my eyes pinned to the date.

The acolyte raised his brows, and I amended it: "Peranza."

The acolyte's brows jumped. "There was another girl," he said. "Who had a sister named Peranza..."

That snapped me back to reality. "I don't know what you're talking about," I said. "I'm an only child."

"Mmmm. Peranza. If you follow me, you can have this date. And more. Much, much more."

My father didn't want this, and neither did I. Frost wasn't in that temple either.

But I was so, so hungry. And Vri was safe, off the island.

I watched the acolyte's back until he reached the top of the stairs. Then it was as Frost said back in the market—the drive to survive took over. I put my foot on the step.

"Peri," a voice said near my shoulder. "I don't think you want to do that."

I didn't have the presence of mind to be startled. Somewhere in my head I recognized the voice as Frost's, but it didn't seem strange that he should have followed me here and finally come to speak to me. It felt like the conversation had conjured him up.

I didn't turn my head. "In the alleys, the acolytes come for the girls with honey pastries. And apples and flatbread and skewers of lamb. Not just a single date."

"Come with me, Peri. I'll feed you." He put his hand on my arm. When he began to pull me away, I did turn to look at him.

His hood was like a tunnel. All I could see was his face—his green-gold eyes, the ruined bones.

The acolyte's footsteps halted. "You, there!" he said. "Don't hamper a volunteer for the dragons."

Frost kept his head down and bowed, like any respectful freeman would. "No, ser. My sister's a little off in the head. She wouldn't make a good Dragon Girl. She's just in it for the food."

He took my elbow and began steering me away.

"You know, they have wine, too," I said. "And if you're deemed worthy, you sleep on a feather bed. In the morning, they serve you mulled cider and sausages and griddle cakes with dates and cream."

"They do not. It's all a scam, Peri."

"Peranza!" the acolyte called, his sandals slapping against the steps as he ran after me. "Let go of her!"

"My father said I shouldn't go with you," I said as Frost dragged me into a stumbling run. "He was afraid you wanted me for the temple. To give me to the dragons. But you aren't part of the temple, are you?"

"No."

"Come back!" the acolyte called, and Frost ran faster, forcing me to run to keep up with him. "Peranza!"

"They'll give me something to eat before they give me the test," I panted. "Even if I don't pass it."

"Not pass it?" Frost scoffed, jerking me into an alleyway between the buildings of the Governor's Office.

"I'm just the daughter of an herbalist. They'd find out soon enough I wasn't fit to become a Dragon Girl. But after they fed me."

"There are many things wrong with that thinking, Peri," Frost said between his teeth. I jerked my arm out of his and made him stop. "*I'll* feed you," he said in an urgent voice. "Now come on, before that acolyte has Granthus's guards after us."

"If you want something out of me, you'll be disappointed. There's nothing left to give."

He looked troubled. Then a shadow swept over us. A big black shadow, like a cloud. But a cloud never moved that fast. We stopped and looked up.

A dragon shot through the air above the temple.

❦

THE DRAGON'S SCALES GLEAMED BRONZE IN THE sunlight, and its fluttering mane and feathered wings were a handsome golden color, the same odd shade as the flecks in Frost's eyes. The dragon screeched and shot upward, knocking over stalls and tables and chairs with wind from the downbeat of its wings.

Then it dove, coming right toward us.

People around us screamed and ran, but I hardly heard them—fixated as I was on the sight of the enormous and beautiful predator hurtling toward me with its teeth bared, fangs exposed, poison dripping from their curved tips.

Frost cursed and stepped in front of me. It seemed a pointless bit of chivalry, considering the size of the dragon. But he stood his ground. He put his hand up and spoke a string of unintelligible words—or maybe I just didn't hear them in the panicked din of the street.

The dragon pulled up, tossing its head. Its nostrils flared, and it bellowed.

Frost said something else. The dragon's neck curved as it drew its head back. I couldn't tell if that meant it would strike or retreat.

Then the acolytes and their guards spilled out of the temple. Before them, they shoved a line of young men and women, dressed in flimsy white robes. Some of them were trying to break free, to run back to the temple. The dragon jerked its head around to look at them, then like a diving falcon, lunged toward them with shocking speed.

"*No!*" Frost cried out.

But it was too late. The dragon snatched one of the Youth, a girl, in its blocky jaws, and turned its head up to choke her down whole. Its gullet convulsed, and I could see her shape against the skin of its throat.

The warriors among the acolytes swarmed the dragon with swords, and it pawed them aside with a single swipe of its huge, taloned foot.

Men screamed, and there was blood on the ground.

"We should do something," I said, looking wildly at Frost. "There must be something to do."

"Hide," he said grimly. "Once the process is started, it won't stop."

"What process?"

"The dragon's enthralled. They've snared it, and there's no way I could free it."

"Why in the depths of the underworld would you want to *free* that creature?"

"I would have explained it to you if you'd stayed with me at the tavern. Now we have this!"

"How can this be my fault?"

"It—dammit, I'll explain later."

The acolytes were trying to rope the dragon as it fed on the other Youth. I had never been this close to a dragon attack, and I had never seen anything so horrible. None of the books I'd read had prepared me for the sight of such a thing—an odd, giant combination of lizard and bird that impaled human beings like mice on poisonous fangs the length of sword blades, then ate them like an eagle swallowing its prey.

Frost yanked me away. "It'll run out of food. If those idiots don't kill it soon, it will rampage."

"If you've got some sort of magic that will turn it away—"

"I told you it's enthralled, didn't I? It doesn't matter what kind of magic I have. It's an animal. Survival instinct. What animal would willingly starve itself?"

He pulled me down an alley, and the scene of carnage disappeared from view. All I could see now was the dragon's head lifting in a sinuous curve over the roof of the buildings as it reared up on its hind legs. Its wings rose and fell, and I could only imagine how many people were thrown about and crushed.

Then the dragon lifted off the ground, snapping the ropes the acolytes had bound it with. It broke free and rose into the air...

And a row of archers on the roof of the temple loosed a volley of fire arrows at it.

The feathers on its wings caught fire, and it screamed. Beating its wings only fanned the flames. Fire ate its way greedily to the dragon's body.

Arrows continued to rain down on it, sprouting from throat and breast, until—still on fire—it bellowed in pain and shot off toward the sea.

"It won't make it far," Frost said. "Poor bastard."

CHAPTER 5

I FOLLOWED HIM, TREMBLING, TO A SMALL ROOM in a run-down boarding house, the kind where men brought their whores. I balked, but he gripped my arm tightly, steering me inside and up the stairs. I swallowed my fear for the promise of something to eat and an explanation.

The room was at the end of the hall. It had a window which looked across the roofs to the pinnacle of the Dragon Temple and beyond, to the mountains capped in snow. I looked for the dragon, but couldn't see it. In front of the window stood a small table with two chairs, and not two steps away, a single cot in the corner.

The room was too neat, as if no one lived in it. A knapsack on the bed was the only sign of a human presence.

Frost closed the door behind us and threw the bolt. Then he crossed to the knapsack and began pulling food out of it. A bottle of wine. A round of bread. A waxed packet of dried meat. A handful of nuts.

One small red apple.

Despite the carnage I had just witnessed, my mouth watered so badly it hurt. I put my hands over it.

"Sit down," he said. "Eat slowly. Or you'll get sick."

I all but fell into the seat, and then I fell on the food. I grabbed the bread first, tearing off a big hunk and setting into it like the dragon had gorged itself on the Youth.

Frost sat down in the other seat. "Slowly, I said." He scooted the rest of the food away from me.

"Do you work for Granthus?" I said, my mouth still full.

He laughed. It wasn't a nice laugh. "Me? Work for Granthus? You mean like one of those idiots in their wooden masks, shaking their bells like a circus monkey? Or like one of those rich acolytes throwing girls to the dragons? That could have been you, you know."

I dug my thumbs into the bread and tore it apart, forcefully. "Only if the magic tests don't matter."

"Would it have been worth it? For a single shriveled date?"

"Maybe." I shoved more bread into my mouth. "As long as they fed me before I had to take the test."

"You're slipping, Peri. If you'd done a little digging, you'd have found out that the Temple takes anyone who comes, even if they fail the test. They cruise the alleys, looking for the hungry and homeless, the people nobody wants. But why are you so sure you'd fail?"

"Because it was my sister who inherited all of my mother's magical ability. Not me. I'm the one who takes care of things. She's the one with the talent."

He eyed me curiously. "Peranza the Steadfast?"

I shrugged, eyeing the food he was still holding hostage. "The Temple came to our door one morning. They didn't try to lure her in, they just wanted to take her."

On a blue-skyed spring morning, back when we had lived in a snug little apartment above my father's apothecary shop, and I could go to the Lyceum and read as many books as I wanted, whenever I wanted. The same morning my father had lost the ability to use his right side.

I swallowed, hard. "They left me alone. I'm not worth it. It's just the way things are."

He eyed me skeptically. "Just something you accept?"

"What benefit is it to anyone if I don't? I'm not Talented. I'm a good scholar, I write a fair hand, and I'm here with my father. Somebody has to take care of him, and I'm the only one he's got."

Frost pushed a cup of wine at me and another piece of bread to dip in it. I latched onto both with slightly steadier hands.

"Your name is not *just* Peranza. You're the daughter of Ximus Kares. The Governor's herbalist."

I couldn't deny it. "Papa worked for the Governor a long time ago. Before..."

My voice trailed away, and I made no effort to finish the sentence. Instead, I dipped the bread in my wine and ate half at a bite.

"*Slowly*," Frost said again, with more emphasis. "Do you want to get sick?"

"Now you know who I am," I said, "why don't you tell me who you are? *Frost* seems unnecessarily dramatic. The acolyte said your first name was Stefan."

"Feeling more yourself now?" he asked with a hitch of his brow.

I laughed. Bitterly. "Quite the opposite. I'm not feeling myself at all. Peranza Kares does not encounter dragons at close range. Or follow strange men into boarding houses."

Now his mouth quirked, too. "Because she's too good for them or because she's never had the chance?"

"Well, both actually, but I'm not keen on getting knifed or raped. I don't know what you intend after this food's gone—"

"What's wrong with your father? Is he sick? Is it fever?"

"No. It's... a wasting sickness. It struck quick. Without warning."

While I was sneaking Vri out the back door. I'd always wondered if my father had brought his injuries on himself, by taking a poison as a distraction, but I had no proof for that.

"Ever since," I continued, "my father has trouble speaking and thinking, and the muscles on his right side are weak. He can't use his right hand anymore." I took a drink of wine that in my current, starved state went straight to my head, and I looked up at Frost. "His face, his eye... it's somewhat like yours."

I had a sudden, irrational desire to touch the corner of Frost's eye, to feel out the similarity, to note the abnormalities. To see if what had happened out there in the temple square was real or dream.

Fortunately, I hadn't had enough wine.

He flinched all the same. His head swiveled toward the window, leaving me only a view of his brown hood. "It's probably not like mine," he said softly.

Then he turned back to me and slowly, he pushed his hood down.

◈

His hair was not entirely white, as I had imagined it. Instead, it glinted faintly of pale gold. He'd cut it short, against the Eterean fashion, and it stuck out in wild spikes until he lifted a hand to smooth it down. His injured eye stared at me with the same odd intensity as the other, and I wondered how he could see out of it, as extensive as the damage must have been. Perhaps some thought his injury made him ugly, but I didn't.

"If your father earned his eye because of a sickness, he's not like me at all."

"Then what happened to you?" I asked.

He leaned back in his chair. "The usual. I had a run-in with Granthus's soldiers. They beat me, I ended up with this eye."

"What do you mean, the usual? That doesn't happen to people every day."

"It does where I come from."

"Where is that?"

"Small village, north side of the island."

"What's on the north side of the island?"

"A small village," he said, with an amused twist of a smile. Then the smile disappeared. "It's where the Etereans landed when they first came. The first place they established a garrison."

"It's been three generations. Why are people still being beaten?"

"Do you think every islander approves of Eterean rule, even now? What's it brought us?"

"That *is* sedition. Saying it out loud like that. If the guards heard you, they'd haul you away, and me, too, for listening."

"So, I should just accept the way things are? Out of fear?"

"You didn't protest when Granthus had that man ripped apart," I pointed out.

Frost looked troubled. "There was nothing I could do in that moment. Not without giving either of us away. But that doesn't mean I accept Granthus's government."

"A group of scholars attempted to write to the Emperor," I said, in a slow, calm voice. The voice I used in debates. "To request another governor. Perhaps the Emperor is still considering. All we can do now is try to survive. Dragon attacks *are* decreasing. In spite of today."

"Maybe. But in the process of getting rid of the dragons, he'll kill us all."

I'd thought that myself, but hearing Frost say it made me uneasy. "You throw your opinions around with wild abandon," I said.

"Do you always talk like you're writing a report to the imperial court?"

"Are you always so careless with your words?" I retorted.

He rested against the back of his chair and folded his arms across his chest. "I like to live on the edge. Saving women from the Dragon Temple, telling the truth, that kind of thing. What were you going to say to me before, when I asked about your father? Something about his years in the Governor's Office?"

I swallowed. As hungry as I was, the bread still felt like a lump in my throat. "It was just a long time ago, that's all."

"You were going to say, *before he fell out of favor*, then?"

"No," I sighed. "I was going to say, *before my mother left us.*"

Frost looked confused. "You mean she died?"

"No, I mean she ran away. With an Eterean Fixer who built machines. Who also worked for the governor's office." I gave him a tight smile, but my hands began to tremble again, so I closed one of them over the apple. Its skin was smooth beneath my fingers, except for a small dent I felt out with my thumb.

"How old were you?"

"Eight."

I desperately wanted to eat the apple. But I couldn't. I was thinking about my father, remembering how he had come home from the office that day, whistling as he walked into our chambers, only to find Vri and I on the couch in our sitting room, alone.

No one there but the cat, who was no help with Vri at all.

"My sister was six," I said, not knowing why I was telling this story to a stranger, but feeling the need to say something. "My mother left us alone in our rooms for the day, saying our nurse would be by soon, but our nurse never arrived and Papa was at work. Vri was frightened." I exhaled—a sort of laugh, maybe. "I spent hours playing string games with her, trying to teach her how to make cat's cradle. It was the only thing that distracted her, and only because she was so upset I could do it and she couldn't."

"Your mother worked with the Office, too?"

"If you know so much about me already, why are you asking me questions? How long *have* you been watching me? You knew about my father from the first, didn't you?"

"Your father's been missing for a long time, Peri. I didn't know he was sick. I didn't know who you were when I began watching you. After we met at the tavern, I started asking around, and that's when I found out you were his daughter. People know you."

"As an herbalist's daughter, that's all. They don't know who he is, and they wouldn't regard me in the same light, anyway."

"I wasn't looking for him or you, exactly. I saw you in the marketplace, and you seemed... competent."

"Until I got caught stealing, you mean."

"That's just odds. You steal enough times, eventually you'll be caught. It's like playing cards. You can't win all the time."

"Well, I'm not my father. Or my mother. Or my sister. My father was brilliant, magic apparently loved my mother so much it seduced her, and my sister..."

I sighed and stared down at the apple. I heard Frost's clothes rustle as he moved, and then he touched my shoulder. I looked up at him, and he dropped his hand.

"Come with me," he said. "Bring the apple."

WE RATTLED UP A NARROW STAIRCASE TO THE ROOF. From up here, you could look over the whole city—a jumble of flat rooftops, buildings like a child's blocks, all the way to the foot of the mountains. Beyond the walls and the docks, black slivers of beach pushed out in fingers between groups of rocks that looked like knuckles. The blue sea rushed up in white breakers, smashing in great sprays against the rocks, then sucked back out again, revealing more flat plains of black sand.

The dead dragon lay at the line between sea and land like a new landform.

"What do you think they'll do with it?" Frost asked me.

"Do with it?" I asked. "What do you mean?"

"Will Granthus do anything with the dragon? Will his acolytes? Or will they leave the body there to rot?"

"What else can they do? It's a dragon!"

"You're starving." Frost jerked his head toward the dragon. "And that's meat."

"But it's impossible to eat dragon. The meat is poisonous."

"That's what they'll tell you. Just like they'll tell you that if you become a Dragon Girl, you'll be a hero."

"The Youth distracted the dragon."

"They gave the dragon an easy lunch. That's different."

"So, what do you serve with dragon? Red wine or white?"

Frost shook his head. "Eat your apple and I'll tell you a story. It starts *once upon a time*."

I studied the sheen of the apple, trying not to feel guilty about not taking it back to my father. If I only ate half of it, I could bring the other half home and cook it until it was soft enough for Papa. I bit into it and chewed slowly, savoring its crisp, juicy flesh.

"So, a fairy story," I said. "No evidence, no facts, just another inspiring legend."

"It's about dragons."

I gestured with the apple. "Well, carry on then. If it's about dragons."

He replied with a hitch of his brow and leaned against the low wall that formed the railing of the roof.

"Once upon a time, a sailor fell in love with a slave girl. The sailor was from somewhere off the charted maps, far to the north where men and women had hair the color of coins, gold and copper. The girl was as poor as the dirt of the island on which she'd been born. She served a harsh but important master, the commander of a regiment of soldiers. He was an unkind man who fell into bad tempers when he drank, but he kept her fed and she had no way of knowing that she deserved more, because this life was all she'd ever had.

"But the sailor knew. His ship was dry-docked in the harbor all winter, the crew guests of the commander's regiment. The commander gave them rooms in the fort in exchange for providing extra defense. The sailor had a lot of time to observe the commander's woman. He saw how she cringed when the commander raised his voice, and he saw how whenever she was near him, she folded in on herself. And he saw, too, that when she walked in the garden, she opened up like a flower.

"The sailor started taking odd jobs around town. He already had some money saved up, but he worked hard to make more. And just before his ship was due to sail, he approached the commander.

I want to buy your woman, he said. *The one who braids the purple orchids in her hair and walks in the garden. I know you have other women, dressed in silk from Saien and gold from Dakkar. But this woman, you clad only in linen and wool. Surely you can let her go.*

"The commander looked at the bag of money the sailor held out to him. Then he laughed and knocked it out of the sailor's hands.

You think a fish gutter like you could afford any of my women, even the lowliest?

I think she's worth more than I could ever give, the sailor said. *And I know she's worth more than you, too.*

"That's a good way to get yourself a beating, isn't it?" I said. "Why didn't he drop to his knees and beg?"

"I doubt that would have made a difference," Frost replied. "The commander was the kind of man who only wants something when he knows another man wants it. The woman was like a trophy to him."

"What did the sailor do?"

"He did what you'd expect."

"He went back to his ship and wondered forever how things would have turned out, even after he got married and had a family?"

Stefan gave me an odd look. "What kind of woman are you?"

I took another bite of apple. "A realistic one."

"He came back that night and stole her away. Snuck her onto his ship and they sailed in the morning."

"Good planning," I allowed. "But what about the commander's guards? How did one common sailor evade all those guards? Are you sure you have all the details right?"

"Yes," he said. "I have all the details right. They snuck past the guards with the help of an herbalist, who concocted them a potion that put the guards to sleep."

"Kacin perhaps?"

Stefan shrugged. "The important part is they snuck past the guards and onto the boat, and she sailed away, free."

"Except she didn't escape on her own. Another man rescued her," I pointed out. "Did she feel the same way about him as he felt about her, or was she simply doing what she had always done? Was she just a survivor?"

For a moment, Stefan looked troubled. He turned his head and stared out over the building block city. The wind caught his short hair and ran its hand through it, mussing it up, giving me a good view of the scarred side of his face.

He would have been handsome before his beating, I thought. Not perfect, like the statues that lined the drive to the Eterean palace, but perfection was so bland, so suspicious. It was difficult to reconstruct what he might have looked like before Granthus's soldiers had destroyed his bone structure, but I thought I could see the lines of it, strong and spare, like the mountains beyond the city gates.

"Perhaps at first," he said. "Perhaps she went with the sailor because she couldn't stand to stay with the commander. But after she spent time with the sailor, I believe she came to love him."

Something about the way he spoke caught me. "Is this a story?" I said. "Really?"

"Of course it's a story. A fairy story. You said so yourself."

"Did they live happily ever after? Then I'll know it's a story."

"You don't think anyone lives happily ever after outside a story?"

"Honestly? There's not a lot of evidence for it. But go on."

"Well, the sailor and the slave girl lived on ship for a while. The ship took them around the world. Eterea, Dakkar, Tiresia, Kavo, Qalfa... even Saien. The slave girl saw wonders she never knew existed. But the farther she traveled, the more homesick she grew. And as she journeyed farther and farther away from the commander, a desire grew in her, a desire to have a family.

"Her baby was born in a storm off Thunder Cape. The boat tossed to and fro, and her screams were drowned in the sound of the storm. But when it was all done, mother and son were both healthy. Only, the mother was done with sea travel. *Take me home*, she begged her sailor husband. *Please. I want to see the mountains again. I want to feel land beneath my feet. I want to raise my son where grass grows green and flowers sprout from the clefts in the rock.*"

"*You know we can't go back*, the sailor said. *The commander may still be looking for you.*"

"*Why would I want to go back to the garrison?* she said. *I want to go home, back to the hills.*"

"So, because the sailor loved her, he gave up the sea. They retreated into the high mountains, since they couldn't live among the people of the coast for fear of being captured. But the mountains were harsh, watered by springs of magic, full of dragons and other monsters, and the land was shit for farming."

I wrapped the apple carefully in my handkerchief and stuffed it in my pocket. "I told you I didn't believe in happily ever after. Either they starved to death, or the commander caught her."

"You did. And yes, the commander found them out."

"Did he take her back?"

"Not exactly. Her husband died, securing her freedom, and she lived on her own for a while, bringing up her boy. They had no money and were forced to live among the hazards of the magic springs. When the boy got older, he got it in his head that the commander was the one keeping his mother hungry and in pain, worn out with work. And so, the boy went down into the city."

"And what happened with him?"

"He was beaten, thrown out, left for dead."

"But he survived."

"He did. Only because they took him back up to

the mountains and dumped his body before his mother."

"So, she saved him? Nursed him back to health?"

"No. She thought her boy had died because of her, just like her husband, and she killed herself."

The brutal spare way he said the words made me pay attention. It was like watching him put his hood down.

He began speaking again without looking at me. "When the boy woke up and saw his mother, dead, he wished he had died. He wanted to die. But something inside stopped him. He couldn't get up, but he was very hungry. The only thing he found to eat was a dead dragon—a small one, just created—by the side of a spring where he crawled to drink."

"He ate the dragon?"

"He was driven to survive. Like any other animal."

"But... an animal's only in it for itself," I said. "The boy could see what pain his mother had been in when she thought he was dead. He wasn't motivated by his drive to survive at all. It was the drive to take care of things. Things that had been left undone and needed doing, not for himself but in love of another. In his mother's memory."

The wind rippled the hood of my cloak and scruffled through the trees that leaned over the roof.

Frost put a hand on my shoulder and squeezed it lightly. I looked up at him, startled, before I realized that it was a companionable gesture, given for comfort. It had been a long time since anyone had reached out to me like that.

When I began caring for my father, it used up so much of my time and vitality I had none left for interacting with anyone else. Half the people we knew escaped the island when they realized where Granthus's policies were headed, and the other half drifted away because I didn't have time to sit in the cafes and argue philosophy like I used to.

Fair-weather friends, my father used to call them.

But Stefan's touch on my shoulder told me he understood. There was such a thing as a drive to care. No matter what the cost.

Maybe sometimes it felt like a drive to obligation—like being crushed in a room that was slowly closing up on you like a tomb. But it kept you going when you thought you couldn't go on. It was not as simple as repaying love given to you. It was not the happily ever after of a fairy story.

It was love, though. A mess of complications, of chains and freedom, laughter and tears, anger and hope. Revenge and maybe redemption.

My father sitting on his cot while the girl I had

paid with a stolen turnip spooned a thin vegetable broth into his mouth.

I needed to get back to him.

Stefan dropped his hand.

"Will you come with me?" he said. "I'm gathering people. To solve the problem of the dragons."

"You know how to keep them away?"

He exhaled, then leaned on the wall, looking into the distance toward the sea where the dragon lay, a swarm of gulls picking at its flesh.

"The problem isn't the dragons, it's what Granthus is doing to keep them away."

"So, what's the solution then?"

"That's easy. Get rid of Granthus."

CHAPTER 6

"I can't be involved in sedition," I said as I clattered back down the stairs. Stefan followed me, his boots thumping heavily on the buckled wooden boards.

"Why not?"

I whirled around to face him. "Because of my father, dammit! Where am I going to put him? Who will care for him? I don't have time to foment a rebellion!"

"Bring him. We'll care for him."

"*We?* You've got a whole village of Seditionists?"

"Something like that. In the hills."

"You're putting an awful lot of trust in a woman you just met, telling me that."

"But I know who you are."

"That's *blackmail*, holding my father's safety over me like an axe!"

He scowled. The expression turned his face into something dark and ominous, even dangerous, but then his anger lifted. "I'm not going to threaten your father, Peri. I meant, I know you, I know your background, and I know you're not the kind of person who would put your father at risk. And more importantly, you just keep going. You have that drive, whatever it is. Peranza the Steadfast."

I shoved open the door to the small room, where all the food was still set on the table. "You don't need me, Stefan. You need someone who can wield a blade, or Shape, or See."

"We need an herbalist."

"Oh," I said, wondering why I sounded so bitter. "So, you did need my father."

My bag sat on the floor beside the table. I bent down so Frost wouldn't see the tears forming in the corners of my eyes and picked it up, then began putting the food into it as carefully as I could with my hands shaking.

"You need to eat more of that," he said.

"Maybe when I get home."

"If you never feed yourself, who'll take care of your father?"

"I said, I'll eat when I get home!"

Stefan took a step back. "It's your choice, Peri."

"It's not a choice!" I said, stepping closer to him, like I was pressing an attack. The gold in his eyes crackled like sparks, and I realized what I was doing and took a deep breath. "It's never a choice," I said in a quieter, bleaker voice. "Not for the steadfast." I picked up my bag and headed for the door.

Stefan grabbed me by the shoulder. "Peri. The meat. That's for you."

I jerked away from him. "We'll see."

❧

I didn't want to do it, but Stefan didn't seem like a man who would take no for an answer. And I didn't want him following me around anymore. Somebody would notice, and then they would come for my father. They would drag him back to the Governor's Offices and use Truthseers to pry all his knowledge out of him, and then Granthus would turn it against all of us—poisons and potions in the prisons, herbs to increase the magical attraction of dragon sacrifices, torture, manipulation. They would leave him an empty husk and then throw him away as if he were chaff beaten from wheat.

I had again paid Yula to stay with Papa, and again, her man the copyist at the Office of Sedition had come to visit her. I could hear their conversation and laughter through the door. I wasn't surprised—it was the only way the two of them got any privacy, even if it was relative—but today it was a stroke of luck.

Not that it felt lucky. Instead, I felt oily inside, as if maybe even my thoughts had left stains. But I went through with my plans anyway.

"Bero," I said as I stepped into the room and unwound my scarf, hoping I remembered his name right. "I want to report a man for sedition."

YULA AND BERO HAD DRAGGED THE ONE CHAIR AS far away from my father as they could get. Yula was sitting in her man's lap, and he had the bodice of her tunic half-unlaced. It looked as if Papa was asleep, but it made me angry to see them taking advantage of the situation like this. When the copyist heard what I said, though, he stopped in surprise, then set Yula on her feet and stood up.

"You've run into a Seditionist?" he said in surprise.

I nodded. "I'd like to report him. Will you get a bonus for bringing him to justice?"

"Yes!" Bero said. He scrabbled through the mess of paper on the table, finally coming up with a blank scrap, quill, and ink. "I'll take your writ right here," he said. "Can you give me a name? Or just a description?"

For an instant, I panicked. I thought about Stefan standing on the rooftop with the wind ruffling his strange spiky white hair, showing me the ruined side of his face like an offering of trust. I wondered at what point in the afternoon he had ceased to be *Frost* and had instead become *Stefan*.

But I couldn't afford to risk my father, no matter what my own views or desires might be. It made me feel hollow inside, and somehow smaller, to do it, but I gathered my resolution and ground out the words.

"Stefan Frost."

Yula's man looked up at me in amazement, quill still poised over the paper. "He's wanted by Granthus himself. By the Guard."

Damn. Now I did balk. Considering the reaction of the acolyte at the temple, I should have known that Frost wasn't a small time political agitator. I wanted to hassle him, not condemn him to the executioner's block. Or worse, to the arena to fight off monsters to prove his innocence. Surely my responsibility to my father didn't mean I had to condemn another man to death?

I stuttered. "I only heard a rumor. That he might be in the Temple District. It's just hearsay, but I thought I ought to say something."

Bero was nodding as he wrote. "Yes. You've done the right thing." He looked up at me when he was finished and grinned. "I imagine he has a bounty on his head. Probably over five hundred astra."

"Oh!" Yula exclaimed, clapping. "Maybe we could even afford a bit of mutton!"

Bero leaped out of the chair and spun her around. Her skirts swished against the legs of the table in a blur of red and blue. "One day I'll be able to feed you all the mutton you can eat, when we've gotten rid of all these damn Seditionists and the dragons."

"Lamb in roast garlic sauce!" Yula exclaimed, laughing. "Meat pies! Pork skewers! Figs and apricots!"

"And only the finest of wines to dip our bread," Bero said, planting a big kiss on her forehead. Then he hurriedly rolled up his paper and stuffed it in his cloak.

"Thank you, sera," he said to me, dragging Yula along with him as he headed for the door. "This could be my big break, maybe I'll even gain a promotion..."

They all but tumbled out the door. Bero slammed it behind him. I winced at the sound and turned to check on Papa.

He was sitting up on the bed, watching me out of shadowed eyes.

"THE BREAD MAN? YOU SAW?"

I sat down beside Papa and began taking every-thing out of my bag except the meat. Stefan hadn't told me what the meat was, but I thought I could guess.

"Yes," I said.

"Peri!"

"Papa. He saved me from a dragon attack. He gave me something to eat. But he wanted something out of me that I couldn't give. The risk was too great."

Peranza the Steadfast.

I winced. My conscience had woken and now it cut into me, but I tried to tell it that this was about survival. Papa's survival.

"Dragon attack?" Papa asked in alarm.

"I'm *fine*, Papa." I hesitated, smoothing my tunic over my lap. "Papa... your work for the governor's office. Did it involve dragons?"

"Governor." His brows pulled downward, at least on the left side, but I couldn't tell if he was angry or merely confused.

"When you worked with Mama."

"Your... mother."

"Do you remember?"

Papa sighed. "She always wanted more. Dragon magic."

"How could Mama have dragon magic? It belongs to the dragons."

He shook his head—or what passed for a shake of his head, a few twitches. "You assume," he said and tapped my head with the index finger of his left hand. "Dragons. Not born."

"If they're not born, then how do they exist? Are you saying somebody *makes* dragons, Papa?"

"Trans—trans—*transformed*. Ordinary creatures. By *pure* magic."

"But how? A Fixer would still have to use magic to—"

"No. *No.* Wild magic. Comes up."

He made a gesture with the fingers of his left hand like water spraying up out of the ground, and my own fingers, which had been pulling at a stray thread, stilled.

Frost's story about the boy who was beaten and woke near the spring, to eat the dead dragon. How had he worded it?

The first thing he found to eat was a dead dragon—a small one, just created—by the side of a spring where he crawled to drink.

Created. Not born.

Frost knew about dragons. He hadn't been

subtle with that story. He was the boy. But now everything made sense.

Dragonmeat wasn't poisonous; it was transformative.

How else was he still alive? If he had been beaten so badly his mother thought he was dead? It must have been the magic at work.

If it had worked to heal him... maybe it would heal my father.

I reached for the pack with trembling hands. "Papa," I said, "I want you to eat something..."

"Ate up your mother," he said, still shaking his head mournfully. "Always wanted more. Ran experiments. To mimic effects. Experiment with you girls too. Gods forgive me."

I stopped, gripping the strips of dragonmeat tight in my hand. "Experiments?" I said, stunned almost speechless.

He sighed and leaned back against his pillows. "Kept her away from Peri. But Vri... too young, liked sweets too much. Why would Dea go that far? My *daughters*."

Now both corners of his mouth almost matched— both of them tugged down, hard. His hands trembled.

I didn't want to upset him more, but I had to know. "Mama was feeding Vri magic in her candy?"

"Candies. Cookies. Custards, puddings." He

tried to smile at me—tightly. "You—never a sweet tooth."

"I ate cookies. Why didn't Mama try harder with me?"

"Vri... much more ordinary."

"No, Vri's the special one. She always has been. More beautiful, more talented, full of..."

Magic. My voice trailed away.

"She ate cookies," my father said, looking up at me with an expression in his eyes as if he was pleading with me to understand. Then he went on.

"Dea wanted... wanted to *prove*..."

He stopped, anger sparkling in his eyes as he wrestled with his brain to produce the words.

"Even the *most* ordinary. Would rise." His shoulders sank with release from the effort. Then he shook his head. "You... Peri. Never ordinary."

I stared at him, waging my own battle with language and memory.

"Papa! How *could* she?"

"Tried—"

"If it worked so well, why didn't she give it to both of us?"

He glared at me and spluttered, chopping the air with his left hand. "Not the point! False magic. Just —a—likeness. With..." A long pause, and his features twisted with effort. "*Consequences.*"

"What kind of consequences?"

"Dragons. Begin as birds. Lizards. Snakes. Rabbits?" He wheezed a laugh to himself. "Maybe rabbits. Need magic. To maintain—form. The springs. Dammed..."

The Etereans and their northern garrison.

I bit off a curse.

There were places in the island's interior, in the mountains, where magic was said to well up out of the earth in springs. It was rumored that the Etereans had discovered such a place and used it to operate their machines, like the ones Granthus used to quell the food riots.

"What do they do if you dam up the springs?"

"Not born with magic. Must have it... from outside."

"Vri and Mama couldn't have been the only new sources of magic," I said. "Nor me, as little as I ate."

"Dragon Girls," my father said in a raspy whisper.

"What?" I said. I felt stupid, unwilling to put two and two together even though I knew they added up to four.

"Dea took girls. Boys. With that Fixer." He spat the last word, and his face contorted. "Bait."

Did Frost know that my own mother had created the Dragon Youth? Was I the only one who didn't?

And still I wanted to know the real answer,

though I despised myself for it. Even without knowing that she had used us for her own dark ends, I'd written her off. If she didn't want us, why should I want her? I'd already cried all my tears, alone at night after the chores were done, the books read, and Papa and Vri were asleep.

But it was easier to say, harder to do. There was still a wound, one that would never heal enough that it couldn't pop open at the least provocation.

I took a deep breath. "Papa... if she was using us, why did she leave?"

"Had an argument. When I found what she was doing to Vri." He closed his eyes. "Then I found out what else. She had become... half dragon, I think."

"So, she really ran off with the Fixer?"

My father nodded. "But best keep it quiet. Granthus—won't like it. That his solution is the problem."

I thought of the woman dying for the figs, the girl the dragon swallowed, the men and women whose lives it had cast aside with its talons.

I thought of the morning Papa lost the use of his right side. When the acolytes from the Dragon Temple had come for Vri to make her into a Dragon Girl and feed her to the dragons, and I'd bundled her out the back door of our tidy house on the good side of town and into the arms of the man who wanted to marry her. The man who took her away from this place, from this pain, from these memories.

I thought of Stefan.

"Papa!" I said. "How could you keep quiet? We're all starving so Granthus can drive the dragons away! But he's drawing them to us instead!"

Papa looked up at me, his dark eyes rheumy with pain but lucid and familiar for all that. For once, the damage to his face made sense with his expression —the deep hurt, the deep pain, the deep love.

He touched my cheek.

"Two girls. No one to care for them but me."

CHAPTER 7

I KNUCKLED MY HAND AGAINST MY MOUTH AND stared at him. His words echoed around my skull, so much like the words I'd spoken to Frost this afternoon.

Frost, whom I'd turned in for sedition.

I dropped my hand and took a big breath.

"Papa," I said. "I'm going to give you something. And I want you to eat it."

I leaned over and opened the pack Frost had given me. My hand shook as I unwrapped the strips of meat.

Would the wild magic differ from my mother's fake magic? Would it still call the dragons, or was it better than that?

It was a big gamble, but I thought I was right. And in this moment—sitting here with him in the tumble of our cold, cramped basement room, with the faint, thin smell of boiled vegetables hanging in the air though they had all been eaten by someone else — I was tired of hiding. Tired of skulking around the edges of life, tired of being quiet, tired of *starving*.

And tired of carrying around this burden my mother had laid on me long ago.

Though I now knew why my mother had lavished Vri with sweets and treats, it still hurt. It hurt in an even more ironic way. Because I had always thought I was the ordinary one—that Vri was special, that she was talented and unique, the one worthy of being saved. When I was a child, I had eaten jealousy like the sweets my mother fed to my sister. I swallowed it all down, where it sat like a ball in my stomach, undigested, unacknowledged.

I had always tried not to hold it against Vri. Because, dammit, she had asked for none of it, and she was not the sort of child who lorded it over her solemn and un-fun older sibling. But Mama's actions had eaten a canker in my heart, and the way Papa treated Vri hadn't healed the wound.

And now I learned that I hadn't even been able to succeed in ordinariness.

I wanted to lie down on my cot and laugh until it turned into crying.

But I had responsibilities to fill first. I was Peranza the Steadfast, wasn't I?

"Papa," I said again, going down on one knee before him. "I'm going to feed you some of this meat. I think it might make you well again, or at least better, but I don't know what effect it will have, truly. It's dragonmeat."

He looked up at me, squinting. "Dragon... meat?"

"Stefan Frost gave it to me. The man who saved me from the dragon. He ate it and it healed him."

Stefan had turned a dragon—a huge, hungry dragon—away from me. A man who had just met me. While my own mother had apparently used my sister and I and our entire city as a scientific experiment, in service only to herself.

I couldn't let one more person be hurt because we were trying to survive.

"Peri. *Consequences.*"

"Papa, this whole situation was caused by people thinking of nothing but their own self-interest, twisting love so it had no choice but to be crushed beneath their heels. If anything will solve this problem, it will be something wild and freely given. Now hurry. There's something I have to do as soon as I can."

"What is it?"

"I betrayed an innocent man. And I'm tired of living under boot heels. Take the meat, Papa."

Hesitantly, he moved his left hand. I put my hand on his before he could take all the strips.

"Not all of them," I said. "Leave some for me."

❧

I DIDN'T KNOW WHAT TO EXPECT. IF THE DRAGON magic would begin working on my father immediately, if it would take a while—what it would look like. I knew from my reading that wild magic could be as dangerous as a wild animal, but now that my father had told me his secrets about my mother, I questioned everything I had ever read about magic and dragons.

And I was ready to stop all these lies. This false plainness I'd been carrying around for years, as if I was always *adequate* but never truly good *enough*. Dependable, but never special.

Well, I was done with that.

My father looked down at the meat in his hand and slowly put it in his mouth. As he chewed, he closed his eyes, and an expression of bliss crossed his face. He'd barely eaten half the strip when it dropped from his hands and he sank backwards into the pillows. A soft glow began in his fingers and spread up his arms.

I would have been alarmed if not for the peaceful expression on his face. Whatever happened, at least I had given him a moment of relief.

I pulled the covers up and re-wrapped the remaining strips of meat, then jammed them into the pocket of my cloak.

"Sleep well, Papa," I said, and leaned down to press a kiss to his forehead. Then I ran out of the room and up the stairs onto the street.

I RAN AS FAST AS I COULD TO THE BOARDINGHOUSE where Stefan had taken me that afternoon, praying the soldiers hadn't moved that fast, and that if they had, that Stefan had moved faster.

But none of my prayers were answered. They were dragging him out of the house, his hands manacled behind him. Blood dripped down his face and stained his white hair red and pink in streaks. Even from this distance, I could see the blue-black sigil the Guard's Fixers had scrawled onto his cheek to bind his magic.

I had to do something. But what could I do?

I did the only thing I could think of. I took the meat out of my pocket and pushed it into my mouth.

It was sweet and spicy, like an explosion at first, then deep with foreign, smoky notes, and a burn like whiskey as it slid golden down my throat. It nestled warm in my stomach, and then the warmth spread out into my arms and legs. I stretched out my arms and wriggled my fingers, feeling the power come into them.

Across the court, Stefan raised his head and turned toward me.

"What are you looking at?" the guard standing in front of him said, tilting forward on his toes. "Are there more of your kind over there? Think they'll save you? Ungrateful prick."

The guard raised his fist to backhand him.

The power was coursing through me now. Magic I had never experienced before. Wild, like the sight of that dragon hurtling through the air—beautiful and dangerous.

I raised my hands and power shot out of them.

I can't describe what happened in that moment. I saw Stefan's cat-green-gold eyes, though I stood too far away. I saw the gleam of dragon scales and feathers in the sun, though the sun had almost set. I saw fire leap up in the courtyard, though there was no fuel to light.

Fire roared through me. I burned up in its heat and anger, turning into a column of pleasure and pain. I let it loose on the men who had brought me to this point, blasting them with flame.

Was it me or the dragon?

Did it matter?

The bodies of the guards turned to ash and fell in fluttering gray flakes to the ground.

The sight took the heat out of me. The magic cut off suddenly, and I wavered like the last bits of ash falling down.

Then, I, too, fell.

❧

PERI, PERI, SOMEONE WAS SAYING. *PERI, OPEN YOUR eyes.*

I blinked. I was on the ground. I felt raw inside, like I'd been scrubbed out with a coarse brush. Standing over me was a man with white-gold hair and eyes the color of a summer meadow. He had bruises on his face, but he smiled.

"I see you ate the meat," he said.

EPILOGUE

What does dragon taste like?

It tastes like spring sunshine on the rocks where I sit by a pool of frothing magic, watching as gulls land only to fly away with beaks full of silver teeth and wings of gold. It tastes like the cold, sparkling spray that spangles the coat of deer who come to drink, only to run away with strange bronze racks of antlers and wings sprouting from their sides.

It tastes like the sight of my father, walking down the path and smiling at me, Stefan walking beside him.

My father isn't entirely healed. He limps and shambles like Stefan does, especially when the weather is damp. His smile will never be the same.

But we're here among the dragons. We're here where we can grow our own food—or steal it from the Etereans. We're still hungry. Still poor. Life is hard in these stony hills. The pool of magic we've been able to liberate from the ground is small. But we don't have to be quiet anymore, here outside Granthus's grip.

Stefan and I sit on the rocks sometimes, wrapped up in cloaks against the cold, and we look down on the city still victimized by Granthus's mad desire to keep everything locked under his control—people, magic, dragons. We watch as dragons cruise by the upthrust towers of the Temple towering above the other buildings—watch them dive for Youth who continue to die in vain, treated like so much meat.

It's hard, sitting. Watching.

But that's not all we're doing now. I no longer huddle hidden in a basement, afraid to be seen, starving.

One day, the dragon fire will come for Granthus, too.

THANK YOU FOR READING!

Thank you for reading *Dragonmeat*! If you enjoyed this story, please consider sharing a review wherever you enjoy talking about books!

If you'd like sneak peeks into my current projects, including upcoming books in the Eterean Empire series, subscribe to my mailing list at Angelaboord.com and receive the free Eterean Empire short story, "Roses in Winter"!

ACKNOWLEDGMENTS

This story was a long time in the making. It began with an idea I had while I was reading the picture book *St. George and the Dragon* by Margaret Hodges to my older kids when they were small. I wondered what happened to the dragons after the knights slew them. Did the carcass just sit around rotting? That seemed wasteful to me—and also to the character who walked into my head not long after, a man who said his name was Stefan Frost.

So I owe a debt of thanks to Margaret Hodges for this story (and, if you have young children, her picture book *The Kitchen Knight* is also wonderful.)

I also owe a debt of thanks to the other authors in the *Dark Ends* anthology—Justine Bergman, Luke Tarzian, Clayton Snyder, Krystle Matar, and D.P. Woolliscroft—for nudging this story into being. Without them, it would just be a few paragraphs scribbled in blue ink, gathering dust in my closet.

Many thanks are also due to my inveterate beta reader Fiona West, especially for helping me refine Peri's voice.

And as always—thank you to my family, who don't complain that half the kitchen table is always occupied by manuscript print-outs and who are always excited when I'm writing another book.

FORTUNE'S FOOL
CHAPTER ONE

Dragonmeat takes place many hundreds of years before Fortune's Fool, the first book in the Eterean Empire series. If you'd like to take a peek at the twisty Renaissance-inspired world of scheming Houses, mercenaries, and magic that has formed out of the old Empire, the first chapter is included here!

My right arm is made of metal.

A man named Arsenault made it for me, but he never told me its secrets. He didn't have time. He gave me the arm and sent me to safety, then he rode off to die.

My arm shines like silver and withstands all weather and all blows, but it isn't a dead thing. No leather straps attach it to my stump, no belts or buckles of any kind. The metal grows right into my flesh. From the sculpted whorls of my metal fingerprints to the dimple of my metal elbow, it might be the arm with which I was born.

Except that it's not.

That arm lies rotting in a cedar casket in the ground beneath a cork tree, an arm of meat, skin and blood like any other woman's.

Not that anyone can tell I'm a woman. I dress like a man and work as a gavaro, wielding my sword for coin. People know me as Kyris. But the name I was born with is Kyrra. Kyrra d'Aliente, only child of Pallo, the Householder of House Aliente.

My father is dead now, and the name Aliente is no longer my own. I am forbidden to use it, upon pain of execution. I may be the last Aliente alive, but I can't even say so.

The men beside whom I fight don't usually want to know House names anyway. Every gavaro tells his own lies of how he came to this mercenary life. After five years of saying it, I have almost come to believe that my name is Kyris di Nada, and that I sprang full-grown, metal-armed, from the rocky brow ridge of the Irondels.

Kyris No-Name. Of Nothing, Nowhere.

The name with which I was born caused a war. Ask anyone in the city of Liera and they'll tell you,

Kyrra d'Aliente did it. Cutting off her arm wasn't enough. They know whom to blame for the crumbling walls of their once-elegant buildings, the deep pits left by cannonballs in the stone canal moorings. The tumbled brickwork still clogs the canals maintained by lesser Houses, who can't afford to dredge them out.

As if I might have been somehow more than incidental in the great games of the Houses. The Prinze controlled an entire fleet and a quarter of the coastline of the Eterean peninsula. Of what consequence was my arm to them? They cast it aside and trod over my family the way their horses trampled our land in battle.

I wasn't there for the battles. Arsenault asked me to go north to Rojornick, out of Eterea entirely, and I did. Some would call me a coward for honoring that promise. Maybe they're right.

But now I've come home, and answers are what I seek. About the five years that have passed since Geoffre di Prinze staged his first raid on my father's land. About where Arsenault might be, if he's not dead and buried. Information has become scarcer and more precious even than a black-market gun, snatched for a small fortune from under the omnipresent eyes of the Prinze.

Every new fact is like a shining flake of gold glittering in the waters of a stream. I sift through them, examining each with care. Then I tuck them away along with all my other secrets. My sex. My name. My arm.

Like a pilgrim, I come to Liera seeking truth.

❧

A sailor's inn, dockside.

The smell of sweat and perfume, garlic and wine. Glowing orange light and jittery black shadows on board walls, men rattling carved bones in metal cups, swilling wine, kacin smoke swirling white out of worn wood pipes. Light glints off everything: the sweat on the brows of men and women, gap-toothed smiles, silver table knives, the eel-skin wrap of dagger hilts.

"Hey, Kyris!" Shevadzic calls, waving at me from his seat at the kai dahn table. He's been teaching me to play. His Rojornicki accent is somehow comforting even here among my own people; I got used to it during the five years I was away, and didn't realize that I would miss it when I came home. I did a lot of fighting alongside the Rojornicki.

I'm not sure what he thinks about me or if he knows about my arm and or what I'm like in battle, but he treats me with a fatherly kind of respect. Gray salts his red hair.

I thread my way through the crowd and over to

the table in time for the next game. "Kyris," a man sitting at the corner says with a grin as I take my seat. He's wearing Qalfan robes, but he's pulled his headcloths down in a casual manner, revealing a thicket of wavy black hair, bronze skin above a stubbled black beard, and that long slash of a grin he's not afraid to use. "I'm winning too much tonight, and Vadz is putting me off."

"Vadz isn't putting you off, Razi," the man beside him says. The glass beads braided into his black hair tinkle when he turns his head. Nibas and I fought together in Rojornick, where he was one of our archers, but when I switched sides and went over to the Kavol, he left Rojornick and headed south, saying he was done with snow and cold and just wanted his native sunny Tiresian drylands. I was surprised to find that he'd gotten hung up here, but happy to see a friendly face.

"Sure, he is," Razi says. "Or else I'd have enough coin by now to head upstairs and find some company."

"Maybe I should thank Vadz for keeping you out of trouble. Every time you go upstairs, I end up hauling your ass out of some fight." Nibas turns to watch Vadz roll the bones and swears. "Vadz. You're a whore. Look at that shit you just threw."

Vadz chuckles as he takes the handful of trinkets —no coin yet—that the men have laid out on the table. "Shit only stinks when you're downwind," he says, grinning.

The men swear while I study the bones he cast. Kai dahn is a complicated game of interpreting number combinations. Vadz's bones have carvings of women on them, too, which give them meanings I'm still trying to remember.

"Do you understand why I won?" Vadz asks me.

I finger the first bone, which lies on its side, showing both a 5 and a woman sitting astride a horse. "Five was in the first position. A lucky number, especially when seven and nine are in the second and third position and twelve is last. The five can therefore be read as a porpoise, a fortunate animal."

"Very good," he says, nodding. "You have a head for this game."

I shrug. "It's just rules, luck, and a little bit of mathematics. There isn't any strategy."

"On the surface, perhaps," Vadz replies calmly, sweeping his bones back into the cup with the side of his palm. "The trick is to know more about the game than your opponent. There are different interpretations. I could call your attention to the three at the sixth position, which alters your reading slightly. The five is not only a porpoise but a woman underneath: a mermaid." He grins.

I pick up the bone and squint at it. The woman

on the horse is naked, covered only by the fall of her hair. "Five's a woman, I understand, but why the horse?"

"Kai dahn is a game Eterean sailors stole a long time ago, from one of the lost tribes of the Saien. To these tribes, everything had two sides. The other numbers in this cast make the five a lucky number, a most fortunate number. But cast in a less auspicious way..." He shrugs, a little shrug. "Five can be the worst number. It causes a lot of arguments, on ship. Interpretations differ."

"But the horse?"

"Love and death, she comes the same."

I frown, staring at the bone in my hands. Those lost Saien tribes have hit a little too close for comfort tonight. I had the day off and spent it playing cards on the Talos, the street where our contracts are traded, hoping to hear just one mention of Arsenault that gave me hope. But all I heard were the same old war stories.

"Hey, Kyris, you look like you could use some wine," Razi says. "You're off duty, yes? Time to have a little fun."

"I would if I had any coin."

"Vadz—float him a loan, get him some wine. He's going to ruin our night with that face."

"It's more likely to be your fault if the night gets ruined," Nibas tells Razi. "Stop blaming Kyris."

Razi shoots Nibas a sour look, then turns to me. "Live a little every once in a while, Kyris; that's all I'm saying."

"Eh, leave him alone," Vadz says. "He probably did more work than you did today, Razi. At least, I hope he did, because he owes me rent."

He eyes me hopefully.

I sigh. "Haven't gotten paid yet, Vadz, sorry."

Nibas picks up his own cup of wine. "You still working that job guarding that Caprine girl?"

"That...ended," I say. "A fortnight ago."

Razi laughs. "What he's not telling you, Nibas, is the girl decided she liked him. Probably all that yellow hair."

Nibas gives me one of the small curves of his mouth that passes as a smile. "That true, Kyris?"

I shift uncomfortably. "Maybe."

"And her father tore up his contract right there."

Vadz crosses his arms over his chest and shakes his head. "When were you going to tell me, Kyris?" Then he sighs. "I suppose I can float you another loan. But no more after this. What about that other job you've got?"

"Right," Nibas says. "Weren't you looking for a gavaro? The Aliente captain?"

He means Arsenault. I nod carefully. I've invented this job because I need the information, and it would seem odd and dangerous for me to ask for it outright. I'm definitely not getting paid for it, and I'm not sure how many times I can put Vadz off. "You got any information for me tonight, Vadz?"

Vadz shakes the bones in the cup. "Everyone in Liera would like to find that man, Kyris. But he's probably dead. Most of the Aliente gavaros are."

"You still think he died at Kafrin Gorge."

Nibas was in Rojornick with me during the wars, but Razi and Vadz fought in Liera. Both of them heard the stories of Kafrin firsthand. Razi looks uncharacteristically serious, and Vadz shudders and makes a sign against evil in the air before him. "Yes, I still think he died at Kafrin. If I was betting, no one would bet against me. You know what happened."

"But no one could place him there. And his body was never found."

Vadz shrugs. "Doesn't mean his body didn't burn up in the fire. There were lots of bodies and all of them unrecognizable, down to cinders and ashes— not even bones left. Haven't you heard the stories the Prinze gavaros tell?"

I've heard too many stories from too many people. There aren't that many firsthand accounts, and I'm ashamed to say that part of me is relieved when I don't have to sit through one. Listening to those stories is like having a chirurgeon dig at a rotten wound.

But I make myself shrug. There are things Vadz doesn't need to know. "I'm wearing a green armband. I don't get a chance to talk to many Prinze."

"Well, they'd be happy if I could lead them to the Aliente captain, too, wouldn't they? They've still got posters up for him. Ten thousand astra on his head, dead or alive. I'd be a rich man if I turned him in."

"As if you would give the Prinze anything, Vadz. I know what happened to your men in the war."

Vadz leans forward on the table and points at me, ready to elaborate on his favorite complaints yet again. "The Prinze had no call to fire on that ship. We were hauling grain."

Nibas shifts in his seat. "Come on, Vadz. How many times can you tell this story? You were hauling guns."

"But they didn't *know* that, did they? They fired even though I'd begun to run up the white flag. The guns were all hid in the grain. They'd never have found them, and we were carrying injured, too, up to the Qalfans in the Quarter."

"So, why would you turn Arsenault over to men like that?" I say.

"I just wonder why you're so persistent in your search for him. What can he matter to you?"

"I have employers who'd like to know, that's all."

"Caprine? That would make a pickle of the peace accords, wouldn't it?"

"If anyone found out. But my employer isn't Caprine. So, you don't have to worry on that account, Vadz."

"Dakkaran, then, maybe," Vadz says sagely. "Didn't your captain have some link to Dakkar? Guns? Kacin?"

The Dakkarans used to hold the monopoly on the guns they smithed and the powdery white drug made from berries from their jungles, a long time ago. But that was before the Prinze stole both from them.

"There might have been some kind of link," I say, hoping I've kept my voice noncommittal. "Guns, I think."

"Whoever your employer is, he doesn't pay you very well," Vadz says skeptically.

"He's paying me for information, isn't he? I haven't brought him much."

In truth, I've found hardly anything at all. It's as if Arsenault has disappeared from the face of the earth. Probably, that does mean he's dead.

Maybe.

Vadz sighs. "Well. If you could use another job, there's been a man in here. Looking for you."

I'm still holding the bone. I lean the chair up so

the front legs rest on the floor again, and put the bone down. "What kind of man?"

Again, the little shrug. "A gavaro; how am I supposed to know? Qalfan. He looked hard."

Razi perks up and scans the room.

"Did he say why he wanted me?" I ask.

"He told me to tell you his employer wanted to talk to you about a job." Vadz gestures with his cup. "In the back room."

My eyebrows lift. If you have business you want to keep hidden, you can rent Laudio's back room, but you'd better pay him well and hope he walks away.

"The gavaro was Caprine, then?"

"Not Caprine," Vadz says. "Sere. He wore an indigo armband."

I stiffen. Sere are almost as bad as Prinze, except that they've managed to retain their neutrality, with ties to both Prinze and Caprine, the two rival families around which the lesser families flit, hoping to sip of their nectar. Lieran politics are a morass of kin alliances, but when it comes down to it, the most important question is *Do you stand with Prinze or Caprine?*

The major feat of the Sere is that they've avoided becoming attached to either House and instead have grown their tendrils into both.

Nibas gives a low whistle. "Working for the Sere would put you in coin."

"And is this employer in the back room tonight?" I ask Vadz.

He glances at me out the corner of his eye. "Do you see that man standing just to the left of the Marquis painting? He's the one who's been asking."

"Found him," Razi says. "If he's working for the Sere, I don't know who he is."

I try to look up without looking up. The Marquis painting is a painting of a Vençalan nobleman in his boudoir with a courtesan, while Cythia, the goddess of love, looks down on him in approval. Laudio probably got it cheap.

The Qalfan gavaro looks out of place beside it.

In contrast to the lush greens and oranges of the painting, he is one lean, angular expanse of black. Black—from the leather boots that show beneath the hem of his allaq, the body robes that are usually white, to the urqa he wears wrapped around his face and head. From this distance, I can't even see his eyes, the slit in his urqa is so narrow.

Black isn't a color you see often in Liera. It's the color of ravens, of carrion-eaters—of death.

I wear a black cloak and a black-and-silver tunic. Those were the colors of the Rojornicki boyar I fought for, and I still wear them in honor of him.

Arsenault gave me the cloak, but I'm not sure he would appreciate the irony.

But there is a familiarity to the gavaro's stance. He's the kind of gavaro you'd notice anywhere, no matter what he wore. Like he's quick with his sword and knows how to use it. And with his height, he probably has the reach to do some damage.

I push myself back from the table with my right hand, forgetting for the moment that Vadz has seen me most often use my left. Nibas and Razi know about my arm because they've fought beside me, but they also know why I like to keep it secret. Vadz frowns at me slightly, but my right hand looks normal enough when it's gloved. It makes the wrong noise when I bump it against wood, though, not a fleshy sound but a slight metallic *ting*.

I close my fingers against my palm and stand up.

Vadz trades a glance with Razi and Nibas. "You know...the war's over and you're not in Rojornick anymore. Jobs are just jobs. You make your money and you get out."

I pick up my own wine and drain it while I watch the Qalfan. He sees me and straightens. Good. I set the empty goblet down and pick up Vadz's dice. "Jobs are always just jobs, aren't they?" I say, shaking the bones.

"Sometimes, I don't like that look in your eye, Kyris."

I tip the cup, and the bones come rattling out.

A five in the first position again. After that, the numbers are all a random jumble, some of them lying on their sides.

"Dread gods," Vadz says. "I've never seen a throw so bad."

I grin at him. "Death's my job, isn't it?"

The Qalfan gavaro doesn't speak as he walks ahead of me up a narrow staircase to the room where Laudio keeps his books, not to the back room. But he flashes a glance at me before we walk into Laudio's study. He has light eyes but not obviously blue. The way his brows pull down over them when he sees me up close is somehow familiar too.

He hooks his indigo armband with his thumb, and the gavaros guarding Laudio's door let us in.

"Who are you taking me to see?" I ask as we cross the threshold of the doorway. He doesn't answer, just keeps walking past Laudio. Laudio comes half out of his velvet upholstered chair, putting his kacin pipe down on a leather-bound book of carefully penned figures. The gavaro doesn't raise his head until he reaches the paneling at the back of the room.

"Tell your mistress she'll have the Imisi rosé if

she wishes," Laudio says, sitting back down, hands wandering over the cover of the book. The Qalfan —half-Qalfan or a slave, with those eyes—looks back at him and nods.

Laudio bends his neck stiffly but keeps his eye on us.

Mistress, he said.

My hopes die. A man who's looking for me might have been Arsenault at last, but a woman...it really is about a job.

It was probably a stupid hope, anyway. I've been in Liera six months now without a single lead on where he might be, except for dead.

The gavaro pushes the paneling into the wall with the flat of his hand, revealing a swing-door leading to a secret staircase. Clean-burning beeswax candles glow on peeling blue paint, outlined in white—waves for Tekus, the Father God. We're close enough to the water that the passage might once have led to a cave that opened into or above the sea, Tekus's domain. The Etereans riddled the high sections and cliffs of Liera with catacombs and filled them with the bones of their ancestors. Perhaps we walk above them now.

Once down the staircase, the hallway winds around the corner of the building, and the walls become so narrow that the Qalfan's shoulders push against them. He glances back at me once but says nothing. Then out of the darkness ahead of us a door appears, illuminated in yellow light. He raps on it twice before pushing it open.

Mistress.

A woman sits there, waiting for us. The room is over-decorated with gilt and panels painted with scenes of goddesses and carpeted in blue velvet so deep, my heels sink into it. Incense laces the air with the scent of cloves, and the warmth of the fire blazing in the marble fireplace raises sweat on my forehead. My metal arm throbs with the sudden change in temperature.

The woman reclining on the mahogany settee makes the room look tawdry in her simplicity. Her pewter silk gown shimmers in the candlelight, modest and yet somehow revealing the way it clings to her body. A pair of ivory combs secure curls the color of black-cherry wood in a fashionable sweep atop her head. She wears no jewelry but a lustrous pearl choker, probably worth more than five years of my pay. Her blue eyes are the color of gathering storm clouds. She narrows them on me.

I know this Sere. Her name is Tonia, and she used to be Caprine before she married. I can only hope she doesn't recognize me.

"Kyris di Nada," she says. "My Qalfan was right; it is you." She smiles at me, a cold, fake smile, one I saw often enough on my mother's lips as she welcomed our neighbors into the conservatory for tea. My mother fought her own wars, not of swords but of teacups, waged on sunlit afternoons with women who filled their husbands' ears with secrets when they went home.

The Qalfan slips behind her to sit on the floor, legs crossed, head bent.

Tonia notices me looking at him. "He's no matter. I trust him to keep information where it needs to be kept."

His silence begins to bother me. "Is he mute?" I know he's watching me from under the wrapped cloths of his urqa, but I can't see his eyes.

"Falin? No. But he's smart enough to keep his mouth closed. And he's handy enough with a sword to keep you from getting ideas."

I eye her warily. "My friend said you might have a job for me."

"They told me you liked to get to the point. Yes, I have a job for you. But surely, you'll let me entertain you first. Will you have some wine?"

Warily, with my hand near the hilt of my sword, I edge over to a chair covered in claret velvet. I sit, and she pours wine of the same color—not the rosé —into a crystal goblet.

"I do have a job for you," she repeats. "But I must know that you'll say nothing to anyone of what is said here. I've heard, through various channels, that you're good at keeping secrets, but I need assurance. You must not speak of what transpires tonight. Is that clear?"

Her gaze meets mine again.

I set my glass down on the table between us. "Do you think I'm that stupid? You've brought your assurance. If I refuse to accept your offer, you'll have me killed before I leave the tavern."

Tonia arches an eyebrow. "You can always leave now. Before you hear what I have to say. But there's a great deal of coin involved."

I'm only too aware of my purse hanging limp inside my cloak. But this won't be a simple matter of guarding a few bolts of silk. Not if Tonia di Sere is in charge of it.

"Coin's not all I care about," I say.

"I've heard that you like to take jobs based on ideals... of a sort."

My right hand twitches and my fingers clack together, softened by the leather of my glove. I clench it into a fist and pick up the wineglass with my left hand. "I wonder who you've been talking to." I drink quick, the way a man might. When I set the glass down again, only a small puddle of red swirls in the bottom, the color of blood.

"I have my sources." She adjusts her legs under her skirts and smooths the fabric over them. "I also hear that this job may appeal to you on a somewhat baser level."

She sips her wine and watches me over the rim.

Something in the way Tonia looks at me makes me think she knows who I am. And wants to use me.

I have been used before.

I stand up. "You can keep your gold and your wine and your Householder intrigues. It's a mess to get involved."

"Don't be a fool. You must have known what was at stake when you learned I wanted to meet you in the back room. You did know where my Qalfan was taking you, didn't you? Or have you been gone so long that you've forgotten the ways of Houses?"

I was right. She knows who I am.

She knew I wouldn't be able to resist a job handed out from the back room of Laudio's, and maybe she also knew the kinds of questions I've been asking. But a job based on the tangled skein of loyalties lying in wait for me here in Liera...

"Keep your House ways," I say. "I'm in for something more honest."

I start for the door. The Qalfan rises in one quick motion, but before he can reach me, Tonia blurts, "Cassis di Prinze is at the Aliente hunting lodge. And I want you to kill him."

"Cassis di Prinze?"

Is my voice steady as I say his name?

Tonia flicks her hand at me. "Go ahead. Walk out that door. My gavaro won't kill you. Maybe you can even see what Cassis does to my family this time. You once had Caprine ties, didn't you?"

"Once," I say, dropping my hand from the door-knob. "But your father sat on the Circle that voted them away."

"And given the chance you'd exact your revenge on him rather than Cassis? Cassis has taken my sister to the Aliente hunting lodge; Cassis oversees the Forza and the Aliente estate. You'd walk away from that?"

No. I can't walk away from that.

A long time ago, I fell in love.

Many ladies had run themselves through on this spear before me, but they hid their wounds in lesser marriages or else moved through the temples, the cripple colonies, silent as a winter chill. I paid them no attention. Instead, I played my scales and worked my embroidery obliviously, hating the friv-olous poems my tutor made me memorize about birds and chaste women.

What I wanted was passion.

The summer I turned sixteen, I thought I found

it. He walked in like the scent of orange blossoms, immediate and beautiful. His mahogany hair, the same color as his eyes, was caught at the nape of his neck in a silver clasp, and he wore a silver-hilted sword at his side. Here, I felt, was a man who could do what women whispered about over my mother's teacups, whose touch could burn away the chaste bonds that kept me stiff as brocade.

His name was Cassis. The son of a family that had no business treating with mine.

Prinze.

I move slowly back to the chair with the empty wineglass next to it. I sit down and curl my hands around the ornately carved wooden balls at the end of its arms.

"All right," I say. "I'll listen."

⬧

"Cassis has sequestered himself on the old Aliente hunting lands," Tonia says, rising to pace. "And taken my sister with him. He says he means to have her as second wife."

"And you believe him?" I ask.

"If I did, would you be here?"

"His father will never allow it. But it might be good for you. You're Sere now. Why should it matter to the Sere if a Prinze marries a Caprine?"

Tonia glares at me. "*Second* wife," she says. "If he stoops to that. I am a Caprine by blood and birth, of the main branch, and the wife of a man who lies at the bottom of the sea because of the bloody Prinze; have you forgotten that?"

I haven't. What Lieran could forget how Ricar di Sere died, leaving the Prinze with the sole claim on the gun trade?

I wonder what game Tonia is playing. I've been too long away from the ways of Houses. "If Driese were to marry Cassis, there would be kin ties. The Caprine could buy guns."

Tonia waves my statement away. "At what prices? My father would never debase himself so, and he will never consent to Driese becoming a man's second wife when she could have her pick of suitors otherwise."

Except that the pool from which Driese might choose a suitor has diminished. The loyalty of the Sere, Tonia's in-laws, is somewhat vague, and there are no Aliente anymore. Or at least, I haven't found any yet.

"She could have her pick of suitors," Tonia says again, as if she can read my thoughts. Her expression grows troubled and she starts pacing again.

"I want you to rescue her," she says, without turning around. "Bring her back and kill Cassis."

Do I want to kill him? It's a ridiculous question.

Almost rhetorical. The issue has never been *whether* I want to kill him but *how*. Slowly, with poison? Dramatically, running Arsenault's sword straight through his heart? Or perhaps ironically—using only my right arm to bash his skull in?

The options I've entertained over the years have been endless but never more detailed than in the past year. I've acquired much more experience in killing people, for one thing, and for another, it's not just myself I'd be avenging now. Not just my family.

Because if Arsenault *is* dead, there's no one who had a hand in it more than Cassis did.

But I don't want to look too eager. If I'm to take this job, I need to keep my head.

"Perhaps your sister doesn't want to be rescued. And what will happen when Geoffre di Prinze finds his son dead? Who else knows about this?"

"My sister is a fool," she says, "and doesn't know the import of what she does. Would you tell me to leave her?"

"Perhaps not. But you didn't answer my other questions."

Tight-lipped, she says, "No one else knows. Driese and Cassis escaped in secret. She met him at a crossroads, but it won't take long for either of our houses to discover their subterfuge. As for what will happen after Cassis is dead...I expect that you will be sufficiently discreet that the murder is not trace-able to me or the Caprine or the Sere, and that no one discovers that Driese was there at all."

My brow furrows. "Won't Cassis's retainers know? Or Driese's maids?"

"Driese has gone in disguise," Tonia says. "She sneaked out with the help of one of her maids under cover of darkness, and my parents are trying to keep the news contained to prevent scandal. I assume Geoffre is doing the same thing on his end."

"How do *you* know where Driese is, then? If Driese took such pains to avoid notice and your parents and Geoffre are hushing it up?"

Tonia brings her head up like a nervous horse. "I have my sources. You don't need to know more."

How often have I heard those words? I spin the wineglass with my right hand and watch the way it throws the light back at the room.

"I'm not a philanthropist," I say. "I lost an arm because of Cassis di Prinze. I'd rather not lay my life at his altar, too. How much will you pay me?"

Some of the color comes back into Tonia's face and she smiles.

"I am a Sere," she says. "The regent of my husband's estate, with all his gold at my disposal. I think we can decide upon a reasonable amount."

"Fifty thousand *astra*," I say abruptly. "And we'll have a deal."

The gavaro against the wall jerks his head up. But Tonia never even blinks. She sits back down on her settee and stretches out like a lioness back from the hunt. Triumph flashes in her eyes.

"Done. Bring Driese back to me safe, and proof of Cassis's death, and fifty thousand astra will be a small price to pay."

I'd do it for free, but I should have asked for more. To kill the son of the most powerful man on the Eterean peninsula?

Tonia pours me more wine. I drink it all at once and it goes to my head.

Just like revenge.

❧

Pick up a copy of *Fortune's Fool* to keep reading! Available in e-book, paperback, hardcover, and audio formats!

ABOUT THE AUTHOR

Angela Boord is a hopeless romantic, a nerdy introvert, and the author of SPFBO5 Finalist FORTUNE'S FOOL. She can usually be found with her nose in a book when she's not writing her own dark fantasy epics of hope, redemption, and relationships in all their messy glory. Angela and her husband live in northern Mississippi in a house full of children, books, and innumerable quantities of Legos.

9 781735 944340